The Price of a Princess
Hardboiled Crime Fiction

Other book collections by Arthur Porges:

Three Porges Parodies and a Pastiche (1988)
The Mirror and Other Strange Reflections (2002)
Eight Problems in Space: The Ensign De Ruyter Stories (2008)
The Adventures of Stately Homes and Sherman Horn (2008)
The Calabash of Coral Island and Other Early Stories (2008)
The Miracle of the Bread and Other Stories (2008)
Spring, 1836: Selected Poems (2008)
The Devil and Simon Flagg and Other Fantastic Tales (2009)
The Curious Cases of Cyriack Skinner Grey (2009)
The Ruum and Other Science Fiction Stories (2010)
The Rescuer and Other Science Fiction Stories (2014)
Unusual Plants of the Galaxy (2014)
No Killer Has Wings: The Casebook of Dr. Joel Hoffman (2017)
These Daisies Told: The Casebook of Professor Ulysses Price Middlebie (2018)

Forthcoming titles by Arthur Porges:

Collected Essays: Volume One
Collected Essays: Volume Two

Books by F. W. Thomas (from the same publisher):

Tales From Stonecutter Street (2010)
Star Turns (2011)
The Rising Sap (2013)

Books by Basil Wells (from the same publisher):

Final Voyage and Other Science Fiction Stories (2016)

The Price of a Princess
Hardboiled Crime Fiction

Arthur Porges

Edited by Richard Simms

Richard Simms Publications

This paperback first edition published in 2020

Richard Simms Publications, West Sussex, England

ISBN: 978-0-9930387-4-7

The thirteen stories collected in this volume first appeared from 1960 to 1967 in the magazines *Alfred Hitchcock's Mystery Magazine, Cavalier, Bizarre! Mystery Magazine, Fling, Off Beat Detective Stories, The London Mystery Selection, Adam* and *Bestseller Mystery Magazine.*

With special thanks to Cele Porges and Joel Hoffman.

For more information please visit The Arthur Porges Fan Site:

http://arthurporges.atwebpages.com

Contents

Introduction

Arthur Porges wrote and sold many mystery short stories to the variety of crime fiction magazines that flourished in the post-war era. He was a prolific contributor to such publications as *Alfred Hitchcock's Mystery Magazine* and *Mike Shayne Mystery Magazine*, his specialty being "impossible crime" stories and mysteries that involved ingenious murder methods. Hitting his stride as a writer in the 1950s and 60s, he was in the right place at the right time; his most productive years occurring in the period before most of these kind of magazines ceased publication. Arthur's golden age as a prolific author of short stories ended when the majority of his markets had disappeared. By the mid-1970s, Porges' output had dwindled, partly due to advancing years and, perhaps, the fact that most writers (unless they are Edward D. Hoch or Ursula Bloom!) go through a prolonged spell of intense writing and then naturally slow down.

Although his traditional "locked room" puzzles have been rightly celebrated, a handful of his stories in the crime fiction field were notably darker in tone, involving particularly nasty crimes, hateful villains, and grim plots that involved blackmail, torture and coldly calculated acts of vengeance. This collection, which I have long wanted to edit and publish, gathers together thirteen stories from the 1960s that were written in this vein.

While a few of the tales assembled in this book were sold to the usual outlets, others found their way into a number of the rather risqué and raunchy "men's" magazines, such as *Cavalier* and *Fling*. An unfortunate result of this is that fans of the author's crime fiction would likely have missed these at the time; a real shame as the stories I have reprinted here have much to recommend them. Moreover, I believe they deserve better than being buried in old periodicals and are certainly worthy of another airing. The clever ideas are still there, for sure, but these unsettling tales showcase Porges' astute observations on the crueler side of human nature and his ability to write entertainingly chilling, sometimes horrific stories with skill and flair. Indeed, within the fantasy and science fiction genres, he penned the odd story that could be classed as horror, such as "The Mirror" (1966) and "What Crouches in the Deep" (1959).

Before allowing the stories to speak for themselves, I would like to share with the reader some background information and personal thoughts on a few of them which may be of interest.

I have opened this collection with the noirish, quite brilliant "Heat" (1960). In his final years, Porges remarked during personal correspondence to me that he rated this story highly, pointing out how it not only exhibited an inventive method of hiding a human body, but was also rich in atmosphere, both literally and figuratively. The setting is a small town experiencing an unusually prolonged heatwave, and the plot involves the mysterious disappearance of a young girl. The subject matter, which disturbingly involves sexual molestation, is handled sensitively by the author and I am pleased to include it here for others to appreciate.

The tragic death of a child also features in "Swan Song" (1966), another of Porges' favorites. It's a rare story, given the obscure publication in a magazine called *Adam*, but also in terms of the plot, unusual for the author, which concerns a mission of revenge against a twisted gangland mobster responsible for the kidnap and murder of a man's daughter. In fact, one could definitely class this story as "hardboiled," although in all candor I must admit I use that term loosely in subtitling this book—these are not tales of washed up private eyes, Mafia families, fast dames, and bullets flying everywhere in shootouts. And as for the theme of "Swan Song," Arthur confessed to me that the poignant death of a beautiful young girl is a bit of cliché. As he put it, nobody cares much if it's some old guy who meets an unpleasant end!

A startling and horrendous ending to a human life singles out "The Price of a Princess" (1964) as one of the most disquieting stories the author ever wrote. Appearing in Norman Kark's legendary *The London Mystery Selection*, and never reprinted anywhere else, what an honor it is to republish it here. It is set among the teenage gangs of Los Angeles, where Porges happened to teach mathematics to college students for a time. I once asked him if this story was inspired in any way by that experience, but he firmly and politely denied this. "The Price of a Princess" describes in awful detail a young gang member's fate at the hands of an unscrupulous group of girls who devise a method of killing him that horrifies the social worker investigating the case. This is not a pleasant read—it is hard to actually like a story of this nature—but the dialogue and tension are handled with a deft touch.

Continuing the theme of morally bankrupt women, "Bet with a Witch" (1963) is another story not widely read among Porges fans. The femme fatale that features here uses all her manipulative talents and physical charms to lure a young man much besotted with her into a strange bet, which inevitably costs him dearly. There is a dark heart to this well-crafted tale, reflecting on the theme of fate, which interested the author; after all, his classic fantasy "Third Sister" (1963) featured the three sisters of fate from Greek mythology. It took me several years to track down a copy of this story and I hope Arthur would have been gratified to see it revived and enjoyed by a modern audience. To my mind, "Bet with a Witch" has much of the spirit of "A Price of a Princess" about it.

Now I could go on to wax lyrical about the elegant conte cruel story "The Emperor's Dogs" (1965), yet another yarn concerning a rather excessively disproportionate and ingenious revenge exacted by a bereaved relative against an unsavory character. Or expand on the merits of the tough and grimly satisfying "The Glint," published the same year, in which a bully turned murderer meets his comeuppance. I might write admiring lines about "Too Young to Live" (1963), where a man down on his luck reads an anonymous letter (the contents of the note are only revealed at the end), forgets all caution and thoughts of consequences, and proceeds to enjoy a hedonistic spree involving the consumption of lots of alcohol and indulging himself with rich, exquisite meals. As an aside, Porges was something of a foodie himself, although I suspect he may have disliked my using that dubious modern term to describe him!

However, one more story, "The False Face" (1967), certainly requires a special mention. What appears to be the unexplained suicide of a man who, on the surface, had a wonderful life with apparently all to live for, prompts his father to hire an insurance investigator to find out the reason why, although the former suspects some kind of foul play. To reveal more of the plot details is to ruin the story, but the publication history of "The False Face" is interesting and ended up being the cause of some sadness to Arthur. He sold this one to *Cosmopolitan* and, according to Barry Malzberg, who worked for Porges' agent Scott Meredith Literary Agency at the time, the magazine's proprietors paid him more money than he ever made on any other story. And this to a publication with much prestige and a huge circulation as well. It would have been something of a feather in his cap and a great thing to have on his résumé. Unfortunately, the timing was bad. Shortly afterwards, the title changed editors; Helen Gurley Brown took over and altered the editorial tone. Porges' thoughtful mystery tale had no place in the new-look *Cosmopolitan*, with the general emphasis switched to sex and beauty. The rights were released back to the writer, and the story appeared two years later in the somewhat less prestigious *Cavalier* magazine. But Arthur, despite this consolation prize (as he put it), was disappointed, having wanted to hit the big time and break into the "slicks."

It was subsequently syndicated and reprinted in anthologies as "The |Reason," a better title, in my opinion, which I have kept for this collection. In fact, this alternative title is the one used by Porges when referring to the story in newspaper articles and letters to me. Furthermore, the plot's suicide angle took its inspiration from a Daphne du Maurier short story called "No Reason." It can be surmised that the retitling was an obvious nod to this. Arthur was very proud of this poignant tale and felt that to any sensitive reader it could be described as a horror story, once the investigator's findings reveal the terrible truth.

I will now hand you over to the author and these devilish, wicked stories that have languished for too long in obscurity. I hope they will entertain, in a darkly sinister way, and not give anyone nightmares!

Richard Simms
West Sussex, England
July, 2019

Heat

Horrible weather—crime to match—that's how I remember it now.

It was the all-time hottest, driest summer on record, which for California is saying a lot. The heat was blistering day after day, with crops dying and the ground baked hard. To make matters worse, dirty-grey clouds hovered over the parched foothills tantalizing us with their promise of eventual rain. But a constant high pressure front kept all that potential moisture out of the valley, and every afternoon, without fail, a searing desert wind blew steadily from the northwest, flapping the gay banners on the used car lots.

It was not an unmixed evil, however, that hot blast which continued even after dark. Santa Maria County is the best area in the state for kite flying. With farming out of the question until the rainy months, people were living as best they could off the previous fat seasons, and the usual enthusiasm for kites had become a mania. All afternoon you'd see them dotting the brassy sky, from fifty cent do-it-yourself kinds to the big boxes that had to be snubbed around something heavy if the owner didn't want to go up with them. In that strong, ninety-degree breeze, the most incompetent tyro could have his contraption up for hours. You could tie the fishline to a shrub, leaving the kite untended for weeks, so effective was the steady blast.

There was constant rivalry in design and performance. The kids liked to have fights, Chinese style, with razor blades fastened just below their kites, the object being to cut your opponent's string and leave him holding several hundred yards of tangled nothing.

Among the adults, except for a few perpetual adolescents, it was more a matter of choosing sides and placing bets. For some years most of us had been out of the running, with Doc Polk and Perry Davis far in front. They were handy and ingenious, with a flair for good aerodynamic design. Doc had won three times in a row, and seemed to be acquiring a permanent edge; but after Davis' wife died, the situation changed rather quickly. It wasn't hard to explain. Davis was so lonesome and distraught that he had to keep busy in order to forget. By putting most of his spare time and all his attention into building new and better kites, he soon overhauled the doctor, who had a lot more work to get through each day. Soon Davis' kites were going higher, and lifting heavier loads than Polk's old prize-winners. Perry's latest design, a huge contraption built something like a glider, was due for testing, and those who had seen the thing on the ground guessed it would outperform anything in town by a mile. It wasn't considered polite to get in close when a man made his first trials—that smacked of spying—but no doubt many a curious eye kept tabs, from a discreet distance, on the sky over Davis' little house in the hollow.

It was ironical, in a way, that his success stemmed from the man's desolation. Davis was simply lost without Sheila; it had been a happy marriage, physically and every other way. After ten years, they still held hands at the movies.

Well, that's the way matters stood, one Saturday afternoon. Nothing on anybody's mind but the weather—will that rain never come?—and kites, when Susie Hertz vanished for six agonizing hours.

As sheriff of Arden, it was bound to be my problem, and I heard the news early, without taking the situation too seriously at first. Susie's mother, an overworked widow, sent one of her brood, Wally, a boy of twelve, to report the little girl missing.

"Ma says she ain't nowhere," he told me breathlessly. "She was supposed to come home at two for her piano lesson. It's almost four now."

"Did you look for her?" I asked him. "The girl's crazy about kites, like all of you, and may have forgotten about the music. Never knew a kid yet that *liked* studying an instrument, and she's quite a tomboy besides." I was well acquainted with the child, a black haired, elfin thing with enormous violet eyes and a slender, sunburnt body that was always scratched or bruised. Nine years old, far from a woman, with the fierce independence of a young hawk, yet feminine to the bone no matter how she ran, jumped, climbed, or put the dismayed little boys on their backs wrestling. She called me "Lawman," after her favorite TV show, although God knows there isn't any resemblance, since the star of the show would make three of me, and is stern enough for six. I'm the small cheerful type.

"We've looked everyplace," Wally said. "She isn't around. It's crazy—Susie never hides out. Why, she don't care if Ma licks her or not."

"Who was the last to see her, as far as you know?"

"Mr. Davis, maybe. She was up there to ask about her new kite. The tail wasn't right. He gave her some pointers, and she left. Ain't nothing he don't know about kites. He's a nice guy, too."

Now if there's anything sure, it's that a person can't disappear in Arden. No place to go. Flat country hemmed in by foothills and desert. You're either in the valley, or you don't exist, so to speak. No nine-year-old could tackle the natural boundaries with any success. Susie had to be within a certain, fairly small, area.

I sighed, convinced the child *was* in that area, and that so far nobody had tried very hard or intelligently to find her. Then I locked the office, ruefully contrasting its cool shade with the hot glare outside, and began to investigate.

It seemed reasonable to start with the one who saw her last, so I went to Perry Davis' place. I found him fighting the new kite, bracing himself against its pull, and squinting somewhat dolefully at the sky.

"How's she making out?" I asked politely. "Another whipping for Doc in store tomorrow?"

"Not up to par," he said in a gloomy voice. "I figured she'd try to take me up in this wind, but it isn't working out that way. I must have botched the camber of the wings."

"Too bad. Maybe a few alterations will save the day. Still time."

"Maybe. If the whole design isn't sour." He gave me a quizzical glance, fastened the nylon fishline to the porch railing, and said, "You didn't come all this way in the heat to check up on a new kite."

"That's right. I've a bit of a problem. Susie Hertz seems to have disappeared."

He stared at me blankly.

"What do you mean, 'disappeared'?"

I shrugged.

"There hasn't been much of a search yet, but Susie was supposed to come home for a music lesson at two, and didn't. Nobody's seen her for about three hours. Might mean nothing, and then again … They tell me she was here about one—that so?"

He nodded.

"Any idea what was on her mind that might make the kid hide out?"

"She didn't tell me anything," he said, looking puzzled. "Nothing but kite talk. I told her brother—what's his name—Wally? All the little devils play Doc and me off against each other. You tell 'em to build a kite this way, and they come back, 'But Doc says—' I suppose he hears the same about me."

"When did she leave here?"

"About two—little earlier, maybe. She took her kite and left. I think she was headed back towards town, but it might've been Barden's Hill."

I peered at the little knoll two hundred yards away. Some of the kids liked to fly their kites from there. It looked bare, but the dry brush was thick enough in spots to hide a slight child of nine. A tiny shiver went over me, in spite of the blazing sun. It was as if I had a premonition. A fleeting vision of that gay, vibrant girl lying dirty and despoiled under a heap of brush.

"Is it possible she's hiding in your house—sneaked back?" I asked him. "You do have a basement, I believe."

"I never thought of that," he muttered. "But why—? We'd better have a look, I suppose."

I raised the cellar door, which seemed pretty heavy for a child to handle, and we went down. It was an orderly room, well lit by several dusty windows. There was no possible place of concealment. As a matter of routine, I came out through the second door, which opened to the kitchen. Once inside, it was easy to make a quick but thorough search of the whole house. I even peered under the bed. No Susie. The only thing that seemed in any way unusual didn't register until much later. As I passed the fireplace, I felt a sudden warmth, coming obviously from a small heap of ashes. I paid no attention at the time.

"Thanks," I told Davis at the door. "If she's still not home, I'll get up a search party. She couldn't have gone very far."

"If there's anything I can do ... She's a nice kid."

"Maybe later," I said moodily, and turned back towards town.

When I got there, Mrs. Hertz was waiting, highly agitated, along with a good percentage of the population, about sixty people. The girl hadn't returned, so I organized a house-to-house search. We combed every inch of Arden, and then fanned out towards the few outlying citizens.

We reached Davis' house about two hours later. When he saw us, he tied the big kite to the rail, and quietly joined our party, although he was not the outdoor, vigorous type we needed for this phase of the hunt. There was a grimness about the man, however, that seemed to mean business, and I hated to snub him.

The crowd searched his place again, in spite of my telling them I'd gone through it earlier. There was tension in the air now. This strange disappearance, on top of the heat and dust, was changing the people into a mob, ripe for violence. They streamed out towards Barden's Hill, poking into every pile of brush and yelling the girl's name. But there wasn't a sign of the child.

I had to bring up some unpleasant possibilities at this point. I didn't want to, seeing their ugly mood, but it was my duty. I had to tell them to examine the sun-baked soil for signs of a grave before it got too dark. Not that I really expected to find one; the ground was so hard, it would take a husky man with a pick hours to bury even a small body.

But we spread out again and retraced all the territory, the homes, the yards, the dry fields. Nothing. At dusk, exhausted and baffled, we dispersed temporarily.

Afterwards, I sat alone in my office, chewing a dry sandwich and thinking. Somewhere in the back of my mind a discrepancy existed, ringing a tiny alarm bell to get my attention. I fought to isolate the clue. Finally, I sat up, groaning at my stiff back. I had suddenly recalled Davis' fireplace. That warmth, and the smell of ashes. A fire in this weather? True, some people disposed of odd bits of paper that way, but never inside in hot weather.

Don't misunderstand my train of thought. No body had been incinerated in that fireplace. It isn't that simple by a long shot. You'd need a large furnace and plenty of time. But something had been burned there—what could it have been? I snapped my fingers. Of course! The kite—Susie's kite! It was the obvious way to dispose of that tell-tale item, at least. If I was right, then surely the little girl was dead, and Davis—it seemed unthinkable. Plump, kindly Perry, so fond of Sheila, such a model citizen. I must be wrong. That was emotion; my reason disagreed.

I locked the office, and took off again. This time, feeling a little foolish, I slipped a gun in my pocket. It hadn't been fired in years.

When I got to Perry's place, it was dark outside, and his lights were on, casting a cheerful glow over the porch. The air was still stifling, and the eternal desert wind hadn't let up for a moment.

Davis came to the door at my knock, stepped aside promptly, and seemed to welcome me in. I saw at a glance that the fireplace was now clean and cold. To be sure, he was an orderly man, but this went beyond normal neatness.

"What's on your mind, Sheriff?" he demanded. "The kid turn up yet?"

I hated to tell him my thoughts. I'd always liked the Davises, as had most of the community. To tell a man you suspect him of murdering a child is hardly like reminding him his driver's license has expired. But I had to make a start.

"Mind telling me just what you burned in the fireplace before I arrived this afternoon?"

His gaze flickered briefly, and my own stomach tightened. It was the reaction of a guilty man; I've dealt with enough of them to know.

"Why—" he faltered. "I guess you mean those old papers and things—just receipts, cancelled checks. That sort of thing." He straightened up, and looked indignant. "What are you driving at, Sheriff? I don't think I like this line of questioning."

"I'll tell you," I said slowly, one hand touching the gun in my pocket. "I think you burned a kite—Susie's kite."

I could see little beads of sweat appear on his forehead.

"You don't mean I—" He broke off, wild-eyed, then added hoarsely: "You searched—twice—all of you. She isn't here."

"I know where she is," I told him. "Let's go outside—you first."

He hesitated, and for a moment I expected a fight. Then, pale, he preceded me to the porch. I put one hand on the taut, vibrating string that led up to the pale night sky.

"Pull it down," I ordered him, and he seemed to shrink into his clothes. "Pull!" I snapped, and he dropped to the stairs, sobbing. I started hauling the string myself.

"I never meant to kill her," he whimpered. "But she was going to tell her mother, I—I don't even know how it happened. Since my wife died, I've been so—so damned restless. I'm a warm-blooded man; Sheila used to say I was never satisfied. And this heat, day after day. If only it had rained, and cooled off ... Susie didn't seem like a child—so wild and sweet and pretty. Oh, my God, and I choked her—little Susie ..."

I found the girl where I expected to, tied in a crumpled, pathetic bundle inside the fuselage of the kite. All the vital, elfin beauty was gone now, forever, and it seemed a terrible, needless thing, born of oppressive heat and tension. Davis was still babbling in a turgid stream, all guilt and self-pity.

"Afterwards I knew they'd come looking. There was no time. I was desperate. I thought if I sent her up in the kite, then when they were through with my place, I could bury her at night, and nobody would ever know." He put his head deeper into his arms, and wailed like a hurt dog.

I was sorry for him, and hated him, too. The other people would react only to their hate. I couldn't risk that, so we took his car and drove to China Lake, where I turned him over to the police. He'd be safe from lynching there.

That night the rains came, breaking the intolerable heat; but they were too late to save Susie.

The Glint

Ed Bowen sat at the dusty window of his apartment, and watched Gilly Siebert going down the street. The hulking pinhead, with his shambling walk like a day-old calf, had always annoyed Bowen in the past. He'd felt that normal people shouldn't have to watch the boy, a deaf-mute and retarded, besides. Some day, he often told himself smugly, the kid will run wild, committing murder, rape, and mayhem. After all, pinhead or not, he was sixteen or so, and bound to have swelling emotions typical of all adolescents.

To be sure, Gilly seemed almost unreasonably good-natured. He loved animals, and had gentle hands. If all the other children made fun of him, or used the boy, they had to respect his courage, because everybody knew Gilly would do anything on a dare; anything, that is, except to hurt people.

He was, of course, unable to read or write; and he made only gobbling sounds with his mouth, but he easily followed simple directions given through gestures and suitable drawings. With his capable hands, he could make superior kites and skateboards, too, which gave him some standing even among the normal kids, more articulate and intelligent, perhaps, but not as handy.

At home, he had little for which to hope. Gilly's birth had almost destroyed his father, a clerk of bookish ambitions, who wanted more than anything else a son able to attend college and master such things as nuclear physics, thus bringing Myron Siebert the kudos he couldn't attain on his own. For sixteen years, the boy's father had ostentatiously ignored Gilly, making no attempt either to love or communicate with him. It was as if the Sieberts had no children at all.

Leona, Gilly's mother, was different, both as a woman and as the one who had carried Gilly. She was a grim, angular creature, juiceless, with a mouth so small she seemed to need a shoehorn to eat a pea. But insofar as she was capable of it, she cared for the boy. Completely non-intellectual herself, she didn't grieve over Gilly's illiteracy; instead, she did her best to develop his tactile facility, encouraging him to use his hands as much as possible in creative work.

Ed Bowen thought about these things, well known to the whole neighborhood, as Gilly lurched by. His attitude towards the boy had suddenly changed. This was due neither to compassion nor any sudden growth of tolerance. Rather, he saw in the pinhead, by his very abnormalities, a perfect instrument of murder.

Up to now, Bowen had never killed anybody. But he was into his employers for over sixty thousand dollars, and faced a long term in prison when discovered, as he was bound to be soon, unless, of course, Tim Collier should die. He was the Senior Accountant, and had been concentrating on the books in a way that meant certain trouble. With him silenced for good, it would be possible for Ed to escape the law. The company might be sure he was guilty, but on the surface, without Collier's evidence, either man could be the one. Bowen could brazen it out; there was no way to pin the missing money on him, since it had been spent in circumstances that left no traces. He was a gambler, an unlucky one, but always far from his natural haunts, and with simple disguises such as elevator shoes, a hairpiece, dark glasses, and pads in his cheeks. He'd be bounced, naturally, but that was nothing compared to prison.

Aside from removing Collier, Bowen could think of no other way to avoid conviction. And yet, to exchange a mere embezzlement exchange for a chance at the Death Cell wasn't smart—unless a foolproof killing could be managed. That was where Gilly Siebert came in.

Bowen had never spoken to the boy. He had, it is true, commented occasionally in the liquor store and other places, like the *Tip Top Tavern*, that the kid should be put away before he hurt somebody; but that was all to the good. Not only would Ed be proven a veritable prophet, but also nobody would expect him to be involved with the

22

pinhead. Others had from time to time hired the boy for odd jobs, or had him make their kids a kite, but Bowen had never had such contacts.

Now, however, he had to deal with Gilly, but in secret; and that called for considerable ingenuity. Nor was there much time; Collier was bound to spot some discrepancies in the books any day soon.

The basic scheme was clear and simple in Bowen's mind. He counted on Gilly's inability to refuse a dare, plus another characteristic that many people held to be admirable even in more valuable members of the community. This was the boy's dedication to any chore once undertaken. What Gilly Siebert promised to do, he did, no matter the cost to himself in bruises, broken bones, loss of income, or future embarrassment. When he accepted a dare to pull trick-or-treat on old lady McGonigle, who threw hot water and blistering maledictions at anybody that came to her door uninvited on Halloween, Gilly went through with it, even though everybody knew she had just acquired a large and surly bulldog. The pinhead got well nipped but accomplished his mission, if returning empty handed and drenched, dragging eighteen pounds of nasty canine by one's pants-seat, is an accomplishment.

Again, when none of the other kids dared hop the fast freight except where it slowed on the grade out of town, Gilly actually dropped to the top of a boxcar from Sullivan's Ridge, escaping serious injury by a miracle. But he had been dared, and his honor was at stake. It was to the credit of the kids that they now tended to discourage such challenges as unsporting, because "poor Gilly doesn't know the score—so lay off, you guys!"

With a character like that to work with, Ed Bowen felt he had it made. After pondering a number of angles, he hit on a perfect approach.

There are fake hand grenades for sale at every novelty store; they are used as paperweights, but also serve to scare people who don't have x-ray eyes and see only a deadly ovoid of corrugated metal exactly like the ones in Europe or Korea.

But a solid dummy wouldn't do; Gilly had to be sold on a trick, something funny but harmless. A search of various novelty shops well away from his own neighborhood, and in his pet disguise, finally turned up what Bowen needed, a facsimile grenade that held a pinch of black powder. It went off with a loud pop, showering bits of colored paper. Ed bought two, in case Gilly was hard to convince.

That much was easy, and no risk. Now he had to get the real thing.

There had been a time, five years earlier, when Bowen had joined the National Guard, hoping to use it for political purposes where he worked, since the boss was a colonel. He had found there was study and drill involved, but no preferment at the company, and had soon quit both organizations. But he remembered the Armory and recalled glimpsing racks of guns, mortars, bazookas—and grenades—in the storeroom.

Dances were often held there, the Armory being ideal in terms of floor space, and cheap to rent. On such nights, a lot of people were in and around the building, so Ed could prowl without being questioned. He cased the Armory on a Saturday, when a dance was held, and although he had expected to make only a reconnaissance, was lucky enough to find a side door open. It led to a hall, which led in turn to a storeroom. Both were deserted. Using a thin-bladed knife he always carried, Bowen got into the storeroom. He quickly located the cases of grenades, and looked for an open one. It was best to leave no trace of thievery, even if it couldn't be connected with him. There was a box half full; from it he took, his fingers shaking a little, one of the live and potent metal eggs. Hastily he slipped out, hearing a roar of laughter from the ballroom, locked the door, and slipped away into the night, damp with cold sweat, but exulting. The toughest part, he felt, was behind him now.

It remained only to work on Gilly, and as secretly as possible. Since the boy couldn't talk or write, he was a perfect ally, but Bowen meant to add other pressures as well.

Since the boy didn't go to school, he was in the habit of wandering about the neighborhood, often spending time in the park playground or on the railroad yard. Bowen stayed home from work accordingly, phoning in to say he had a virus. From his window that morning, he watched hopefully until Gilly shambled by, heading for the freight yard. Quickly, Bowen slipped out, and taking back streets easily intercepted the deaf-mute near the dump, where privacy was most likely of a morning.

He smiled at Gilly, who grinned back; his smile, like the legendary one of Davy Crockett, was enough to paralyze a 'coon, but amiability shone through it.

Bowen began by giving the boy a dollar, which generous gift won his regard immediately. He loved chocolate, and no doubt intended to buy some the first chance he got.

Then, Bowen took out one of the novelty grenades. He had removed most of the paper filling in order to add lead shot, since otherwise the thing lacked the heft of a real weapon. Ed pulled the pin, slowly released the lever, and handed the grenade to the boy. He took it gratefully, thinking it another gift. Ten seconds later it exploded, showering him with paper and lead shot, all quite harmless. Gilly gobbled in fright and dismay, but seeing that Bowen was laughing and offering him another bill, he made throaty sounds of glee.

After that, Bowen showed the boy a picture of Tim Collier, clipped from the company magazine. He explained very patiently, with gestures and sketches on a pad, just what he wanted. At five-thirty, he demonstrated with his watch, Tim Collier would leave the office and go down Harper Avenue. Ed showed Gilly a picture of the building. Gilly nodded vigorously, to show he knew the place. The boy was to meet him as he left, hand him a grenade, and wait for the explosion. No, he mustn't run; it was a dare. Play the trick, but don't run until after the explosion. If he did that, and told nobody in advance—here Bowen waved not a mere dollar bill, but a ten-spot. Gilly's muddy brown eyes widened at the tempting sight. Most dares brought him nothing but prestige, and trouble. This was a pleasant change; this was a nice man.

Bowen made sure. He repeated the whole indoctrination. To his surprise, Gilly was not slow-witted after all. His head was just too small for his hulking torso; the kid was far from stupid. So much the better; he would follow instructions, hoping for ten dollars. It was a relief to know Gilly had enough sense to do the job properly, but was still unable to blab about it.

As for the denouement, Bowen didn't much care. People would probably think that the boy found a grenade, a common occurrence judging from the papers, and was moved by some whim to "serve" it on Collier; perhaps Tim just was handy, and it would have been anybody. Or they might figure some kids egged Gilly into it, without themselves knowing the grenade was alive. Whatever their notions, nobody could tie Ed Bowen to Collier's death. And nothing else mattered. Certainly the loss of this pinhead would not hurt society much.

Bowen nodded at the boy, shaking his head up and down to indicate a "yes," a strong affirmation expected. Gilly imitated the motion vigorously; his eyes shone with resolution. It was obvious that the stories were true; what this boy promised to do, he did; you could see the determined glint, all right. It couldn't have come from the wishy-washy father, Bowen thought. Maybe some ancestor had been strong willed, and now his precious gene was futilely lodged in a deaf-mute monster.

Bowen left the boy. It was almost noon. He had stressed not only secrecy, but also the importance of leaving the pin in position until the "trick" was to be played. No point in blowing up Gilly—not alone.

Ed went home as furtively as he had left, reentering by the back door, and crept past the manager's apartment. After that, the hours dragged, the evening seemed a thousand years away.

At five-fifteen, Bowen opened the front window, although it was chilly out. The office was only three blocks away; perhaps one could hear a grenade that far. These new ones, he understood, were a good deal more powerful than those in World War II, some of which were weaker than firecrackers and harmed nerves and ears more than tissue.

Sure enough, he heard the explosion clearly, as did much of the town. Since so many people were hurrying towards the scene, he felt free to join them.

When he arrived at the office, he felt his pulse leap. The ambulance was there already, and two bodies, covered with reddening sheets. His plan, in spite of nagging doubts, had worked perfectly. Tim Collier was out of the way, and nobody could pin a thing on Ed Bowen.

He learned the next day that both victims had died on the spot, riddled by metal fragments. There were dozens of wild speculations going around, but none of them involved a third party. The consensus seemed to be that Gilly had found a grenade and handed it to Collier to scare him. It was obviously an unfortunate accident; Tim Collier certainly hadn't an enemy in the world.

At the *Tip Top Tavern*, Bowen agreed. Collier was a prince, and very competent, too. A drink to poor Tim.

It was several weeks before the embezzlement was discovered. Then Bowen had an uncomfortable session with old P.J., the vice president.

"It had to be you or Tim," P.J. said, "and I know Tim was straight as a string all his life. I've never been very sure of you, but didn't have any proof."

"There isn't any," Bowen said, keeping his voice level. "I'm not guilty."

"That's brave, accusing a dead man."

"I accuse nobody; I just defend myself."

The officer was breathing heavily, his face flushed. "If we go to court, you'll tar Tim Collier, I suppose."

"I'll defend myself," Bowen repeated, feeling a glow of confidence. His psychology had been sound. They wouldn't prosecute.

"You're through here," P.J. said. "Your punishment will come sooner or later, be sure of that. But I won't prosecute; it would hurt Collier's family, and do no good. Some crooked lawyer would get you off. Get out of here, before I'm sick!"

Bowen cleaned out his desk and left. He was tempted to demand proper notice, but decided to leave and then write for two weeks' salary. He'd get it, too; they didn't want to tangle with him legally, that was plain.

When he got home, there was a woman in his apartment. He recognized her gaunt, stringy figure. It was Mrs. Siebert. He felt his stomach contract like a clenched fist.

"The manager let me in," she said. "I said I was your aunt."

"W-what do you want?" he stammered. "I don't know you."

"It wasn't easy to find you; I'm not smart. But finally I thought of the office where poor Mr. Collier worked. I don't know no other place to try. I showed them the drawing. They told me who it was."

"What drawing?"

"My poor boy couldn't read or write—or talk, or even hear. But he was good with his hands, and I got him books from the library, with nice pictures. He was good with a pencil or crayons. See how he did your bushy eyebrows, the bump on your chin, the way your ears bend at the top. At the office they knew you right away, from this."

She held out the sheet; he took it numbly.

"He drew it that afternoon, before doing—doing what you made him do."

Bowen looked at the page of sketches, vaguely aware that Gilly, the deaf-mute, must have been a born caricaturist. Here was he, Bowen, and the undoubted face of Collier, all set out like a cartoon panel, and showing the whole frame-up. The grenade popping to spew paper, just as Gilly expected it to happen; the ten dollars promised, graphic and nasty for him in its implications. But she was a fool, no brighter than her son, to hand it to him like that. He tore it to bits, backing quickly out of her reach, but she made no move to stop him. Instead, she opened her great, shabby purse and took out a heavy revolver, an old fashioned weapon, the horse-pistol type that was popular years ago. Bowen gulped at the sight of it.

"W-what you gonna do?" he quavered.

"Gilly was a good boy, a loving boy; he was all I had. My man's nothing—just nothing. Gilly couldn't talk, but we sat together, laughing, making pictures. He was all I had, and you killed him. Well, mister, I'm going to kill you now."

"No!" Bowen begged, reaching out with pleading hands. Then he saw the glint in her eye, the proof-mark of her iron determination, and knew the source of Gilly's glint.

That was Bowen's last thought. The huge pistol boomed three times in rapid succession.

28

The Reason

Jan van Meter was very rich. He could trace his family back through New Amsterdam to Fifteenth Century Holland. Obviously, Fred Clement thought, such a man didn't have to accept any casual police investigation as final.

"I'm certain that it was murder, and not suicide," van Meter said, his pale blue eyes glowing with conscious power. They had an odd surface sheen like that of polished stone, and stabbed into Clement's mild brown ones. *He doesn't think I look like much*, the insurance detective reflected, with secret amusement. *The old boy can't see that if I had an openly strong a personality as De Gaulle, for example, the little confidences that make my cases work out so well would never be forthcoming.*

Clement was a small, round man, with cheerful, soft eyes; his clothes were of good quality, but just sufficiently rumpled to give most people a fellow-feeling towards him never accorded the impeccable.

"The main reason the police call it suicide," Clement pointed out, "is that he put the gun-muzzle in his mouth. Now, if it were murder—"

"I've read the report," van Meter said, cutting him short, not so much in rudeness as in a businessman's sense of the value of time. "You can forget it. Bill would not, and did not, kill himself. No van Meter has ever done such a thing. He had no possible reason. He was successful, had a lovely wife and two fine children. Believe me, he was a happy man." He jabbed the detective again with his pale stare. "Midwestern Mutual tells me you're their crack investigator. I give you carte blanche. I want the swine who killed my boy. The sky is your limit on expenses; and when you find him—and you will, if it

29

takes years, so don't expect to get off the hook—there will be a sizable bonus above your salary."

"All right," Clement said mildly. "I'll investigate. And as long as I'm here, perhaps you could tell me something about your son: his habits, personality. You know what's useful, I'm sure."

"I'm ready to cooperate one hundred percent. There were no skeletons in Bill's closet. And any in mine," he added, with a touch of grim humor, "are pretty dusty old bones by now."

"You said Bill was happy. Can you be sure of that?"

"Absolutely. He was always a cheerful, outgoing boy: Good-natured. Something of a prankster, in his younger days, but never malicious.

"He married his childhood sweetheart, Moira Drake, had an excellent position as president of Shorwood Valley Bank; taught Sunday School classes, enjoyed hunting and fishing, owned a fine home in Sapphire Bay—why shouldn't he be happy? And his health was perfect; never sick a day. He was only thirty-seven, with a whole life to live. Would such a person, relaxing and perfectly normal on a Sunday morning, suddenly kill himself? Without even leaving a note, when his wife steps out for a few minutes? Police report—nonsense!"

Clement left the van Meter estate in a thoughtful mood. Nobody knew better than he that our society is one of masks and masquerades: that many a seemingly happy and successful person was like one of those fungus-blighted tropical trees—solid and healthy looking, but ready to collapse at a blow, shattering to rotten powder. And yet, so far, William van Meter could not be considered a masquerader. On the other hand, very little evidence was in.

Clement's next stop was at the exclusive Sapphire Bay housing development. It was one of those oceanfront organizations run like a corporation, and very selective in its admissions. All the homes were strictly one-acre minimum, and none valued under $75,000, which, by a curious coincidence, happened to be William van Meter's yearly salary.

If Clement hadn't carried a letter from the elder van Meter, he might never have got past the gate from the highway, which had its own guardhouse and a man in uniform presiding there. The detective's beat-up compact clearly was out of place on the immaculate private road, which wound up and around giving one breathtaking view after another of the Atlantic, a rich turquoise color that sunny morning.

At nearly the highest point, in a magnificent home on five landscaped acres, Clement found Bill's widow. Five minutes in her presence convinced the investigator that if van Meter was a suicide, the motive had nothing to do with his wife. She was not beautiful, but she had a sweet graciousness that went to the core of her being. Her mouth was just too large for her narrow face, but showed tenderness, good humor, and generosity. When she spoke, Clement noted that her voice struck the pure middle note with all the richness of a silver bell, yet with no metallic overtones. No man, he thought, could ever tire of that verbal melody, even if the woman spoke inanely, which was clearly not the case. Deeply feminine, she had the unequivocal frankness of a lady: somebody of so unquestioned a position that no pretenses were called for or even dreamed of. Quietly, she told him about her husband's last morning.

"He was lying on the sofa, reading the Sunday paper. I had been in the kitchen, and remembered that I promised to stop at Sally's—Sally Maitland, our neighbor—and give her a recipe. I told Bill I was going, that I'd be back in ten minutes. He said—" her voice shook briefly—"I grudge every minute, Kitten," and laughed. He had a wonderful, merry laugh, like a little boy without a care, who's watching a circus clown for the first time. We'd been married twelve years, but every day— several times a day—he told me how much he loved me, and what our marriage meant to him. I don't understand," she added, almost in a whisper, "how anybody can talk suicide. Bill had a conscience bigger than himself. He would never do such a thing to his children and me." She sat there in silence, apparently forgetting her visitor.

"You went to the Maitlands'," Clement prompted her softly.

"I'm sorry—I left you for a minute, Yes, I went out. And while I was there—it couldn't have been more than twenty minutes—we heard this popping sound. It was just like Bill's little .22, but I didn't recognize it at all; I didn't dream he'd be suddenly shooting, on a Sunday morning, and around the house. He took it down to the water once in a while, but never near the house. He hated to annoy people, and was very careful about guns always.

"But when I got back—by the kitchen door; and the radio playing some dreadful teenage music—I'd left it on for news, but forgot that when I remembered about Sally and the recipe—when I got back, and looked in on B-Bill ..." She was crying now.

"You needn't say any more—about that," Clement said.

She wiped her eyes.

"I'm s-sorry. Each time I think I'm under control again ... but it's still only three weeks, you see. And it's so hard to believe somebody you love is gone—forever."

Gently, Clement led her to talk about Bill's past; he was soon able to infer that her husband, unlike some, didn't conceal much of his early life.

The family had lived in the east, but Bill had been sent to an outstanding and exclusive prep school in California, Coleridge Academy. He had stayed there, except for vacation visits back to New York, until almost seventeen. Then, anxious to have him nearer home, his parents had enrolled the boy in the Wallingford School, a Maryland institution.

Clement's sympathetic manner, which stemmed as much from his character as his years of experience in dealing with the bereaved, enabled him to get a full account from the widow. It certainly seemed, he thought, as the slow, lovely voice sang on, that they'd had an ideal marriage. If Bill wore a mask, it was a completely new sort in the detective's world. When a man romped with his kids, constantly brought his wife flowers and little surprise gifts, was adored by every child in the community, and always sang—loudly and off-key—in the shower, you had to conclude that as in Beerbohm's famous story, the individual (if ever actually different inside) had changed to fit the false face, and was no longer a mummer.

Well, Clement told himself on leaving, I still haven't left home plate; not even a solid foul to my credit as a batter.

His next call was one of a series made on van Meter's neighbors in Sapphire Bay. Thanks to his letter from Bill's father, and a few phone calls from his widow, people were willing to cooperate. Here again, the verdict was unanimous. Everybody loved Bill van Meter: he was jolly, kind, helpful, wonderful with kids, and, in short, the perfect fellow to have next door. Nothing was too much trouble if it would make things easier for a friend.

Even the community's one malcontent (although the term was much too strong, Clement felt), Louis Busoni, who made it clear that he had a grievance against Sapphire Bay, expressed his approval of Bill. The others, Busoni hinted, backed off a little, more from his foreign name, perhaps, than anything in his character, which couldn't be faulted, since he was not only a distinguished wine manufacturer, but a collateral descendant of the musician. A Busoni, he implied delicately, had no reason to feel inferior to any Cary, Lee, or Fish. But Bill van Meter and his wife had often visited the Busoni's.

"He loved my little Tina," Busoni said. "And she—she's beautiful! So beautiful at eight! What she gonna be at eighteen, I don't know! She was crazy about Bill. And Bill's wife—a wonderful lady, like a great princess, but so kind."

As he drove out through the gate, exchanging friendly waves with the guard (who had melted at the elder van Meter's signature on a pass), Clement began to wonder if it was really suicide. Maybe the old boy had something. A guy fixed like Bill was the last person in the world to make the big jump.

He decided to see Jan van Meter again; make a no-progress report, so to speak. Naturally, it was unacceptable.

"Everything you tell me," the old man said coldly, "confirms my own beliefs—that Bill was murdered. I don't know, and can't imagine why, or how the killer got the gun in his mouth. Knowing my son, I'd say it must have been somebody he knew and liked—somebody, maybe, who told him it was a joke. Bill enjoyed such things. Or used to. He was a lot more mature at thirty-seven, naturally, than at seventeen."

"If it was suicide," Clement said, "then the roots must go farther back. With your permission, I'd like to check into his early life—at the school here, and maybe even the one back in California."

"You have carte blanche," van Meter reminded him. "But I don't think you'll find any murderers at either Wallingford or Coleridge Academy."

"I'd like to agree with you on murder," Clement said. "But you know Sapphire Bay. Bill was alone for about twenty minutes. It has been proved that nobody came near the place. Some kids were playing nearby; a Mrs. Walton was watering across the street; even in back, a gardener was doing some work that morning. What with all those, and the guarded gates, no stranger could have come near Bill, as far as we—the police and I—know. Only Mrs. van Meter. And if you said she could possibly be guilty, I'd have to stick my neck out, knowing how often we misjudge people, and deny it. After seeing and talking to Bill's wife, I can't go for that one loophole."

"I should hope not," van Meter said, stiff with indignation. "If you had suggested such a thing, I'd have had you thrown out of this house. Moira, a murderer, and of Bill! I say again, they were still in love, and happy as mere humans can ever be."

Since Clement had no answer to this, he didn't offer one. As long as the old man was willing to foot the bill, the detective had no objection to further investigation; but the lines must be his own. The murder theory was still cobweb frail, more air than substance, but suicide seemed equally improbable. That left accidental death. But how a man put a gun muzzle into his mouth, directly against the roof, and pressed the trigger—all inadvertently—was something Clement couldn't explain. However, years of insurance work had taught him that nothing was too bizarre to happen to or among human beings, and so he kept an open mind about Bill van Meter's strange death.

The pickings were lean at the Wallingford School in Maryland. Bill had enrolled there, fresh from Coleridge, when almost seventeen, and had left to attend Princeton at eighteen. That was in 1945.

The headmaster of Wallingford, a tweedy chap with an English accent, remembered Bill, and rather to Clement's annoyance, thought highly of him. The unanimity of opinion was no help. (Who ever heard of a guy without an enemy?)

"Very likeable young fellow; well-bred, but not stuffy. Always merry"—that word again, the detective thought wryly—"but never mean or cruel; at least, by intention."

"How about accidentally?" Clement pounced.

"I can't recall any case. Once, I think, he dyed an old lady's dog with a harmless vegetable stain—bright purple. But when he heard that she cried, and thought they'd hurt the brute—actually it was pacified with a hamburger, I believe, and would have been happy to be victimized daily—he sent her candy and apologies; so that later she became quite fond of Bill."

"Oh, brother!" Clement breathed. "This guy can't be for real; he makes Schweitzer look like the Marquis de Sade."

"Not at all," was the chilly reply. "The boy had a Puritan's conscience under the fun loving nature of a—a—" He seemed at loss for a comparison, so Clement supplied it.

"A Henry the Eighth?"

The headmaster's mouth twitched under its neat moustache.

"Not too good a try," he said dryly. "Henry's humor was both brutal and coarse. Quite the opposite of young van Meter's."

So that was that: another fat zero.

It seemed a waste of his client's money, but Clement decided to go west and learn what, if anything, Coleridge had to offer. But first he did some checking at Princeton, learning (without surprise) that everybody there loved Bill van Meter. Even more amazing was the fact that in spite of his money, good looks, and athletic ability (which led to a violent and unrelenting pursuit by all females old enough to wear nylons, and not too senile for hope), the boy dated only his childhood sweetheart, Moira Drake, and later married her on his twenty-fifth birthday, when he was three years out of college, and rapidly rising at the bank.

"Incredible," the detective muttered, studying his notes on the plane west. "Nobody killed Bill van Meter. He was an angel on loan, and Somebody Up There recalled him!"

The headmaster of Coleridge Academy was dead, but his wife was still alive and able to supply a few more facts, all equally bland and useless for Clement's purposes. He heard again the word "merry," and winced. But when she mentioned Bill's best friend, Larry Keith, the detective's attention sharpened.

"Where can I find him?" he asked. "Do you know?"

She didn't, of course; Keith had left a year after Bill; but there were records at school ...

There were good records, but out of date. However, this sort of thing was routine, so it took Clement only forty-eight hours to track Larry Keith down; he was a CPA, and quite successful.

"I've been rather out of touch with Bill," he told the detective somberly. "I couldn't believe it when I heard ... Bill van Meter a suicide. It just doesn't add up. He was such a jolly fellow, if you know what I mean. Loved being alive; got along with everybody. We had a wonderful time as kids. Did one crazy thing after another, but never hurt anybody. The things I could tell you!"

He told quite a few, most of them far from new: the chamber pot on the flagpole; the huge purple shorts on General Wayne's bronze horse; the detergent in the Memorial Fountain—any school paper could supply such a list.

Baffled again, Clement went back east for another consultation with Jan van Meter.

"I knew very well you'd find nothing at either school," the old man said. "Bill didn't kill himself. But you had to satisfy yourself; I don't mind that. Now, however, it's time you changed course and began looking for a killer."

"I'll get to that," Clement said calmly. "But there are one or two things to check—pretty far out, I admit, but possibly related." He didn't explain, and van Meter didn't care to ask. He'd said carte blanche, and usually meant what he said.

The detective found out from Moira van Meter what paper Bill had been reading that morning. He went to the morgue, and scrutinized the issue, line by line. Nothing seemed relevant. Nobody had threatened to "tell all." No skeletons, presumably, had been hauled from closets via newsprint that morning. He'd already verified that Bill had not received a phone call while Moira was out those few minutes. Clement was stopped cold: blind alley, dead center.

He went over his notes again, thinking wryly of the Crofts saga about Inspector French, that bland and competent fellow, not unlike himself, who always re-read his notes when stumped.

There was only one thing left to check, however unpromising. Moira had mentioned leaving the radio on. It was barely possible that Bill, lounging in the next room, had heard something. God only knew what a happy man could hear over the air on a lazy Sunday that would make him put a gun-barrel in his mouth and blow off the top of his head, unmindful of the effect on beloved wife and children, but an investigator must be thorough. One fact overlooked could be *it*. You must never forget that, Clement knew.

He had to question Moira again; luckily, she listened to the same newscaster every Sunday morning; he was an acid-tongued and witty fellow.

Clement got a transcript of his talk. Not a word of it seemed to apply to Bill's action; all international and political comment, venomous, witty—remote from Sapphire Bay.

The investigator went back to his notes, fuming. Nothing there; the field had been reaped to the limit. All right, he told himself: think, man. You're missing something.

Then it came to him—one last angle. The newscaster hadn't quite begun when Moira left. There was an earlier program, a short one of the human interest variety. It should be looked into. Bill could have heard that, too, if listening.

So Clement returned to the station, got that transcript. It read:

Good morning, ladies and gentlemen, this is Joe Satterfield with The Human Angle. I've cancelled my original story for today to bring you an exclusive from the Far West, the little community, almost a ghost town, of Gold Creek, California.

A few days ago, some kids, playing soldier and hacking tall weeds with wooden swords, spotted the ruins of an old car. A little later, getting closer, they also found, to their horror, a human skeleton inside.

Twenty-four years ago, a salesman named Sam Kolitz, was hurrying back from his customers in the east—back to his home in San Francisco. He was really rushing, and I'll tell you why in a minute. It's the pitiful topper to this heartbreaking story.

But, near Gold Creek, the highway was blocked by an accident, a big oil truck jackknifed. Sam Kolitz couldn't wait, and learned about a little-used side road that met the highway farther north. He took it, and vanished for almost a quarter of a century.

Do you know what day it was? They were able to tell from papers and receipts in the car. It was December 6th, 1941. That's right, a Saturday: the one before Pearl Harbor.

And how could a car with a man inside be lost all that time? It's a matter of crazy coincidences. When the blockage was cleared up, very few used the side road. Snow came early, and it was heavy. The war drove casual motorists off the highways, and Gold Creek, the only town near the buried car, lost much of its population to the war-plants.

Then there were mudslides, and finally a huge mass of milk thistle—a terrible weed with murderous spines—sprung up to bar any approach to Sam Kolitz's tomb.

And there's another mystery: why all the bits and strands of rusted wire tangled in the rusty car? Was this salesman, a poor man of forty, robbed and tied with wire—left to die, after he pulled off that side road, perhaps for a nap, which he so badly needed?

Here's the topper. Sam Kolitz was hurrying home because he'd been telegraphed that his little daughter, Linda, nine, was dying. They never got to see each other. Linda died in February.

So far, we've been unable to locate Mrs. Kolitz; nobody knows if she's still alive. The disappearance of her husband shattered the poor woman, and she moved away.

Think of the tragedy. This salesman, trying to make it home, driving day and night. Blocked by an accident, he takes what he hopes will be a shortcut, or at least a way around. He's very tired, so he pulls off that dirt road for a nap. And then—and then, what? A killer? A madman? Or did Sam Kolitz take his own life, unable to go home to face his dying child? Or did he die of natural causes, perhaps in his sleep? Ah, but if any of these, why so much wire, thin, tough stuff, in and around the old car?

I wonder if we'll ever know the true story of Sam Kolitz, who vanished the day before Pearl Harbor, and was found this week, near the little town of Gold Creek, California.

This has been Joe Satterfield with The Human Angle. See you next Sunday.

Fred Clement whistled softly when he read this. Was there a tie-in? It didn't seem likely. Bill van Meter, the callous slayer of a harmless salesman. Quite impossible. But wasn't Coleridge Academy near Gold Creek? Surely somebody there had mentioned the town.

Then a thought came to him, a dreadful vision. Feeling ill, he grabbed a jet, and headed west again. He had to have another talk with Larry Keith.

Keith seemed puzzled to see him again so soon, but quite cordial. Clement wasn't sure how to open the discussion. Did Keith know anything? It didn't look that way. He was ruddy, relaxed, cheerful; no little demon of guilt in his rather bulging grey eyes. A man would have to show some signs of soul damage, *if* he knew.

After some meaningless questions about Bill's life at Coleridge, the detective yawned ostentatiously, and as if bringing up a minor matter of the most casual interest, said: "Mrs. van Meter—Bill's wife—mentioned one prank you forgot to tell me about. Something about a man in a car, near Gold Creek. That's pretty close to Coleridge, isn't it?"

"Car?" Keith repeated blankly. "I don't remember anything like—say!" He grinned broadly, eyes lighting up. "You know, I'd forgotten that one for years. Damned if it wasn't the day before Pearl Harbor. We had plenty to think about on Sunday, and never did check back as planned. But it was a lulu, all right; only Bill van Meter ever came up with such ideas. I wonder if Moira got it straight; it's too good to spoil."

"I'd like to hear your version," Clement said, a cold grue beginning to seize him. "Sounded very funny, what little she remembered." *The hunch was right*, he thought.

"Well, it was Saturday, and we had the afternoon off. It was a couple of miles from school, I guess. Anyhow, we'd found this big spool of wire that must have fallen off a truck from one of the defense plants—stuff for England, maybe. It was real good steel, a kind of heavy piano wire, and plenty of it, too.

"Some kids would have sold it for a few bucks, but Bill was loaded, you know, and my folks weren't poor, either. So we took it along; we were just rambling around; it was pretty wild country then.

"Well, we spotted this jalopy pulled well off the old dirt road behind a clump of eucalyptus trees, and moved in real easy like for a look. There was a guy asleep in the back seat; some kind of a salesman, I think; there were sample cases. He was a fat, greasy looking type, and needed a shave. Snoring like the devil. He was really dead to the world; drunk, maybe; or just pooped. Anyhow, that's when old Bill got this idea. We had all that wire, and so, very quietly, he begins to tie the car shut—no kidding! He wrapped one coil after another around, over, and through, with knots, loops, and tangles until it looked like a fish net. You should have seen the job he did! I swear no opening big enough for a snake.

" 'When he wakes up,' Bill says—the guy was still sleeping like the dead, and snoring real loud; must have had adenoids or something. Funny how I still remember that. And about him needing a shave so bad. 'When he wakes up,' Bill says, 'he'll get quite a shock.'

" 'Sure,' I said. 'But all he has to do is lower a window and start yelling. Somebody will come along and get him out.'

"Bill said that was too easy, and would spoil the effect; so he jams all the windows by pushing little twigs and stuff into the cracks at the bottom—like wedges, you know. That old car was some sight when he got through, believe me.

"Then Bill said maybe it was a pretty low trick at that; not much traffic there, and the dope might be stuck for hours—overnight even—and lose dough. And so, to even things up for the fat peddler, he puts a twenty under the wiper. He was like that, Bill was, full of fun, great imagination, but never out to really hurt anybody, you understand. He figured the guy would be happy to make a double sawbuck from the joke. In those days, that was money. He'd have to sell a hell of a lot of neckties or whatever he had in his cases to net that much dough." Keith chuckled. "Wish we could have seen it. Man, without help he'd still be there! That wire is murder; you can't break it, or cut it with a knife. Only strong nippers can chop up such stuff."

Clement gulped, swallowing a sour spray that came up from his stomach. "You didn't read the papers about three weeks ago, when Bill kill—died?"

"What papers?" He goggled at the detective with prominent grey eyes. "Three weeks ago I was in Hawaii. Sure, I read the papers there, some of them. Why? Something on Bill?"

"Nothing," Clement said. "I was thinking about a different point; it doesn't matter."

40

Keith was obviously in the clear, and not just covering up. A body near Gold Creek would hardly be played up away from California. A paragraph here and there, at most, in a few mid-western or eastern papers. So Keith still didn't know the payoff of that 1941 prank of two teenagers; and Clement had no desire at all to enlighten him. Two deaths were enough, even twenty-four years apart. Not that this fellow was the sort to commit suicide over a joke that went sour; there was complacency in the bulging eyes, a sleek smugness about his whole person that ruled out such an act. And he was only a follower, to be fair.

Clement made a quick exit, in no mood for further talk. He was hardened to his job, and had seen some unpleasant things, and worse people, but this was a bad business. Sam Kolitz, the fat, probably flabby salesman, with bum feet, dead tired on his run home to a dying child, awakening from a much-needed nap to find himself inexplicably wired in, as if some great metal spider had wrapped the car with her steel silk.

At first, there would be astonishment, doubt that he was really awake, and not still dreaming. Then annoyance at precious time wasted by some clown of a practical joker. And—the detective found himself actually shuddering—the beginning of fear as the tempered piano wire resisted all his efforts to make an opening. Apparently there was not even a knife in the car; not that one would help. No ordinary blade would work on such stuff. As Keith had said, it took heavy professional nippers. He'd try the windows, then, planning to yell until somebody heard him and got the needed tools. But all the windows were jammed. It's not easy to break such glass. Maybe he did manage it with something from the glove compartment, or a shoe; but then what? The wire was still there, a tight, small-meshed net; he couldn't break that with a shoe. No, all Sam Kolitz could do was shout. And keep shouting until his voice went.

Then the man must have panicked—but Clement didn't care to pursue the thought. Later, there was heavy snow to cover the car, muffle any cries, chill the life out of the scared salesman. Nobody came by, perhaps for weeks; gas was rationed, the road little used. Then the terrible thistles—Clement had seen them eight feet high; had

41

once laughed at their odd scientific name: *Silybum*. They were impossible to touch or get through, with needles only this side of cactus.

And now, years later, kids hacking with wooden swords; a ruined car with a grinning skull at one window; bony fingers still extended to claw futilely at the wire, finally rusted to pieces.

No wonder that Bill, with a Calvinistic conscience sharpened by responsibilities and maturity, was so abruptly and deeply soul-sick on learning what he'd done to a man hurrying home to a dying child—and Bill loved kids; no wonder, then, that Bill van Meter had to end himself on the spot, forgetting his wife, his own children, everything but the need to erase the searing vision of Sam Kolitz clawing vainly at a cocoon of piano wire.

"And, oh my Lord," Clement muttered, as his jet hissed eastwards. "What can I tell the van Meters—and Moira?"

Was it best, he wondered, to let Bill's death be blamed on an unknown killer, a madman? Or to hope that the family would be consoled to learn that because of a giant conscience he had taken his own life as some kind of amends for a boyish prank believed to be quite harmless? One carried out twenty-four years ago by a kid only distantly related to a family man of thirty-seven. It was a difficult decision to face.

Born to Save

Most teachers welcome the approach of Friday with the fervor of a Dickens character nearing Christmas. Dave Tyler liked his work and his field, biology, but still looked forward to the weekend. In one sense, it was part of his routine, since he used the isolated mountain cabin for research as well as relaxation.

It's true that there aren't many animals a biologist can leave alone and untended for several days at a stretch, but insects did qualify. And his main interest—the huge, oddly gentle tarantulas—were even better suited to such treatment, since they required only a dish of water once a week. As for food, they didn't seem to care whether that came each Friday night or once a month.

Tyler got to the cabin about five, inspected the spiders, which, as usual, were sluggish but definitely alive, and then glanced at some of the other specimens, all in neatly built wire cages. They had nothing to complain of either, since mantises, crickets, beetles, and cocoons are the most undemanding of laboratory insects.

Dave made some coffee, and while sipping the black, strong brew, mentally reviewed his plans for the weekend. More experiments on the intelligence of tarantulas—he was getting remarkable results there; the creatures did rather well in mazes—a bit of fishing, and some really wild stuff on metamorphosis. One cage was certainly ready; a matter of hours, at most.

He was just swallowing the last drop, when a rifle boomed only yards from the cabin. Tyler sprang up, opened the door, and looked around indignantly. What he saw changed mere annoyance into rage. A tame deer, that he had humorously called Mendel, after a famous geneticist, was thrashing convulsively in the clearing. The deer had been shot squarely in the paunch, a stupid and callous operation at any time, but out of season and involving an obviously tame deer, as the collar proved, it was utterly inexcusable.

Then three men—youths actually, although two of them were hulking giants—came into the clearing. They didn't see Tyler at first, but the one with the rifle yelled, "Hey, I got him!" and the smallest echoed, "Vince got 'im. Lookit him kick, will ya?"

Then they saw Tyler. A million words were trying to stream from his throat, but one thought was paramount.

"Finish him off, you filthy devils!" Tyler cried. "Shoot him in the head!"

In a queerly impassive way they studied him, then looked at each other. The doomed animal suddenly scrambled to its feet. Tyler knew that if the deer took off now, it might run for miles before dying in great agony. He started to protest again, but the boy with the gun, obviously afraid of losing his prize, fired again, shattering the deer's shoulder.

"In the head!" Tyler said, almost unable to believe what he was seeing. "For God's sake, in the head—now!" Once more the deer lay there, limbs moving with jerky, uncoordinated spasms. The ground was drenched with blood.

Silently the three youths closed in on Tyler.

"Man, you pass out orders like a sergeant," the biggest said. He stood directly in front of the teacher, looking down at him. The rifleman was now just behind Tyler's right shoulder, and the third boy hovered near his left side. He was boxed in, and he felt sudden alarm. These fellows were obviously not from the small town of Cabrillo, fifteen miles away, but were probably from Los Angeles or Santa Monica.

A horrible wheezing came from the dying deer, still struggling feebly.

"Will you please kill that buck?" Tyler begged. "What's the sense in leaving it like that?"

"Sure, Pop," the boy with the rifle said, smiling coldly. Taking deliberate aim, he gut-shot the deer a second time. "Now ain't that too bad—I missed his head."

"You're a lousy shot," the small one said, nodding in disapproval. "Lemme try."

He snatched the gun, pointed it with great care, and fired into a hindquarter.

"Whaddya know," he grinned at Tyler. "I'm a bad shot, too."

For a moment Tyler stared into the shallow eyes. Then, almost without intending to, he knocked the boy down. At the same moment the deer gave a last bubbling snort and lay still in death.

The boy didn't get up. Instead he watched Tyler with malignant eyes until a hail of blows from his two companions sent the man down to join him. Then he got up, felt his jaw, and kicked Tyler in the abdomen.

"Lay off," the biggest one said then. "Don't mark him up."

"When I get done," the small boy said, "there'll be marks on the marks. He hit me, man—he's gonna pay for that."

"Sure," the biggest agreed, "but there's something else. We killed this deer out of season, and he's a witness. And bein' on parole, you and me can't even carry a gun. Carl here"—indicating the third, silent member of the group—"ain't too clean, either."

"Talk, talk," Carl growled. "You two bug me."

"Carl sees what I mean," the biggest one said. "We gotta shut this guy up."

"I was doing it when you stopped me."

"Sure you was. Then the fuzz find him, all lumps, and start looking around. How do we know who seen us around here?"

"I getcha," the small one said. "We gotta make it clean. But how? Pop here ain't gonna blow away." He jabbed Tyler with a metal-cleated heel for emphasis, and the man groaned, beginning to understand words again after a hazy blackout.

"Joe, you and Carl haul him into the cabin, and we'll see what's there."

"Okay, Vince."

Carl took Tyler under the arms and dragged him bodily, while Joe helped by digging pointed toes into the man's thighs.

By now the sun was setting, and Vince lit the gas lamp on the table. He did it gingerly, not quite sure of the technique, but the device—

after popping loudly—threw a golden glow over table, walls, and floor.

Joe found a cage of beetles, put it on the hearth, and stepped on it.

"Knock it off!" Vince grunted in disgust. "Everything's gotta look natural. Don't go making it easy for the cops, you clown."

Carl dumped Tyler into a chair, holding him down with a hand like a saddle. The boy had flickering, stupid eyes, and they roamed about the room. It was Vince who took the lead again.

"With a gas lamp," he said, "there oughta be gas, right?"

"Over there," Carl grunted, pointing, and Joe scuttled over.

"Here, Vince." He put the gallon can on the table.

"Not so near the lamp!" the big one snapped, moving it to the other end. "What a clown."

"You shouldn't keep calling me that," Joe protested.

"Then quit being one. Can't you do nothing right?"

"What about him?" Joe demanded, anxious to change the subject. Obviously he meant Tyler, who sat there, face expressionless, although he was sweating with fear. At first he'd been afraid of a bad beating. Now he would welcome a few broken bones if it stopped there.

"You saw all those no smoking signs," Vince said. "This is dry country now. If a lot of it caught on fire, and they found his cabin in the middle—and him—they'd figure Pop here got careless. They wouldn't be looking for us at all."

"Vince, you got a head on you!" Joe said, and Carl nodded slowly, his eyes still shifting restlessly.

"It burns too fast," Carl said. "I seen it on TV. We might get caught."

"There's ways," Vince told him. "I know a good one. My stepfather used to start lots of fires—insurance racket, big time stuff. Joe, see if there's a candle in the joint."

"This is crazy," Tyler interrupted. "You can't murder me just like that."

Vince looked at him in silence for a moment, then smiled his cold smile.

"We'll vote," he said. "That's fair. I say we do it to Pop. What you say, Carl? Joe?"

Joe was laughing as he opened drawers and cabinets.

"Real democratic; I like that. I'm with you, Vince."

"We got to," Carl rumbled.

"How about you, Tyler? You got a vote, too."

"Don't do it," the man said thickly. "I'll forget about the deer. I swear it."

"Lemme count," Vince said. "One, two, three for—and one against. How do they say it? The aye's have it."

"Here's some candles," Joe announced. "How many you need?"

"One is plenty," Vince said. He surveyed the room for a moment, then said to Carl: "Tie Pop to that chair, and do a good job. And then tie the chair to that beam so he can't wiggle it near the candle."

"Tie him with what?"

"There's plenty of fishing line in this drawer," Joe said.

"That's the stuff," Vince said. "Use plenty of it." He studied a spool. "Perfect. This kind oughta melt away. No clues even if anybody looks."

"They won't do no looking with the whole damn valley in flames," Joe said. He grinned at Tyler. "Smokey the Bear ain't gonna like you, Pop—setting a whole hunk of forest on fire."

"Cheer up," Vince added. "They'll never convict you."

"For God's sake," Tyler blurted. "Do you kids know what you're doing? To murder a man—burn him alive!"

"Shoot him," Carl said, wild-eyed.

"We can't," Vince told him. "The fuzz ain't crazy. They find a hole in him, and we're done for."

"He hit me," Joe said. "Let the tough guy burn."

For a moment Tyler thought of asking them to put a bullet through his heart, pointing out that no trace would be left in that case; but the urge to live until the last minute was too strong. After all, something could happen to save him. But he knew that was almost impossible. Nobody lived near this leasehold of his; they didn't rent such places in the National Forest any more. Only the old-timers were allowed to keep their own. As a bachelor, he didn't even have a wife to come looking for him, not that she'd have come in time anyhow.

47

Carl had him tied up tight and was now using triple lengths of fishline to tie the chair to the heavy vertical beam. Meanwhile, Vince was soaking rags in gasoline. He was clearly a bit puzzled about the next step. If he put the candle right on the rags, the vapor might explode into flame almost at once. Finally, he devised a wick soaked with lighter fluid, leading to a heap of shredded paper next to the rags. Still not satisfied, he found some kerosene and set up a completely separate lead from the candle.

"This has gotta work," he told his friends. "If it don't, this guy can put us away for a long time."

"Maybe we oughta kill him first," Joe suggested again. "We could choke him—that don't leave no trace."

Tyler's heart was pounding, but he said nothing. With psychopaths like these, any remark might do more harm than good. If you opposed something, then they had to do it.

"He couldn't talk then," Carl said, backing Joe.

"Sure, but if the fire don't work right and they find him, it ain't a deer killing. It's murder, you clowns. We'll do it my way."

As Tyler watched despairingly, Vince broke off the lower third of the candle, and lit the wick. He let several drops of molten wax fall to the floor, then stuck the base firmly in the blob. He carefully wrapped the wick around the bottom, and added kerosene to the second set-up. He eyed the whole arrangement with knitted brows, made some final adjustments, and said: "I figure we'll have at least three hours to get clear. This candle's thicker than the ones my stepfather used, so at least three hours. Now let's move."

"That's a mighty nice gas lamp," Joe said wistfully. "I'd like to take it."

"Okay," Vince said, "but nothing else. They might check up on what's here."

"You don't understand cops," Joe jeered. "They're too busy shaking down gamblers to waste time on a two-bit deal like this." He took the lamp, holding it high at the door as the other two went out. Then he turned to Tyler, sitting ghost-white in the flickering light of the candle.

"So long, Pop. Sorry I can't stay for the big barbecue!"

"Close that window before you go," Vince ordered. "A breeze might blow the candle out."

"Sure, Vince. You think of everything." He removed the prop, slammed the window shut, and locked it. Then he left, closing the door behind him.

For several minutes Tyler seemed to have no control over his muscles. Then panic galvanized him into meaningless action, so that he strained at the bonds, rocked the heavy chair, and finally yelled, hoarsely and incoherently until his throat closed from sheer fatigue.

After that, he calmed down and tried to think of something more constructive. But the simplicity of the trap, plus the double lead to gas-soaked rags, made a solution very difficult to find. If the chair had been free, he might have rocked and eventually tumbled it near enough to the candle so that he could blow it out. But, as it was, he couldn't get near the thing at all. In fact, the only equipment within reach—if anything can be within the reach of a thoroughly bound man—was the set of cages. And the tarantulas, while showing an interesting ability to thread mazes, were not able to untie him, even if they were turned loose.

There were a few tools on the same bench, but they were useless to a man with immobilized hands and feet. In short, as Tyler realized, fighting a new surge of panic, there was nothing he could do for himself. The nylon cords, used in multiple by Carl, could have held a gorilla, and their very thinness made it worse, since the knots were small and hopelessly tight. He watched the candle with feverish eyes, anticipating the terrible moment when flames would envelop the cabin.

Outside it was as still as death, except for the chirp of crickets. The ones inside were answering. Up to now he hadn't even noticed that. Then, suddenly, he was aware of a faint rustling sound. It came from the lab bench, and when he saw what caused it, Tyler could have laughed at the irony of the situation, because it seemed years since the time when that sound might have been the high spot of his weekend here. Now it meant nothing to him. He was going to die, and they—

It came to him then, in a mental thunderclap, that hope lived in a little wire cage. If only he could knock it down, get it to open. Wildly, jerking his body from side to side, he urged the chair to the limit of its nylon tether. It took twenty minutes, but finally he was able to bring the back of the chair against the shelf of cages. It was a sturdy board, a lab-bench built into the wall, but his frantic batterings were having an effect. The tarantulas were full of vitality now, running about their own prison, but he had no eyes for them.

At last the shelf sagged, and several cages fell. The one he wanted most teetered on the edge for a moment, and he rammed the chair sideways once more. The wire container fell, bounced, and to his delight, the top flew off.

The candle was burning too fast, he noticed with new terror. Evidently Vince's experience didn't apply to this brand. There couldn't be more than an inch left right now. And what he longed for might take time. You couldn't ask a newborn child to run …

But these newborn children didn't have human failings. One by one, they fought dampness and flaccidity to achieve fulfillment. Then, bright-eyed and glorious in their fragile beauty, they sought their goal.

Two of them died in vain, but the third great moth put out the candle flame with its body.

The time they bought Tyler was enough. After many hours of effort, he broke free. His first call thereafter, was to the sheriff.

The Price of a Princess

I've been a social worker for thirty years, but this is the end. I can't stand any more. They say nothing has changed; that evil is always the same—no better and no worse from one generation to another. I used to believe that, or tried to. Not now. These children are a different breed. They're not young at all, but ancient darkness masquerading in the bodies of our boys and girls.

Oh, we had delinquents in the Twenties; lots of them. But they didn't start killing at twelve, and their brutalities were somehow of an earthy, ignorant kind, not the cold, sly, pointless sadism of today. Right now I'm bitter over the death of Bobbie Denellan, but that was just the climax; there was plenty before: it's only that I refused to face the facts.

No, I'm through with field work. I'll do my job at a desk from now on, where people are statistics instead of personalities. No more children with adult, nasty faces. If they won't give me an inside classification, I'll quit. I know there isn't much else a spinster of fifty can do after a lifetime in one profession, but I'd wash dishes on skid row before paying another visit to the Princesses or Dukes. All those weary years here in a few square blocks, and what has changed? Only me. I'm dried out, old, tired, and the kids are worse than ever. And now Bobbie Denellan is dead.

I knew him all his life. All his life! And him dead at fifteen. What else was he at that ripe old age? War Counselor of the Dukes. And who were they? A gang of forty-odd boys, ranging from twelve to sixteen years old. They are also the law in this neighbourhood. The Dukes control about three blocks, and as absolutely as any medieval nobleman. After that, their territory gives way to that of the Sharks.

The names they pick! Of course, these are only "social clubs." That's what they tell the police. And God pity any gang member who deviates from that story.

The girls are almost as bad. In Duke territory, their club is called the Princesses. Only about twenty members in that. They're not as violent as the boys, but morally back them to the limit against decent society. It's quite an alliance. Dukes date Princesses, just as Sharks do Belles. When there are police around, the girls carry zip guns and knives for their boyfriends. This makes life hard for the cops, since they daren't search girls without having a policewoman for that job. Never would a Princess date a Shark, because if that should happen, the War Counselors are consulted, and a big rumble, or gang war would result.

Well, Bobbie is dead, and the Dukes will need a new War Counselor. Because of the way it happened, there won't be any war or summary execution. After all, accidents do kill people, even Dukes. If they knew the truth … I've been tempted to tell, but you just can't slough off thirty years of training. For a social worker to encourage violence instead of trying to stop it is unthinkable. Only it isn't to me, right now, because Bobbie Denellan is dead, horribly, cruelly dead, and somebody ought to pay.

I remember him so well as a baby, although that was fifteen years ago. He had the virtues and faults of Irish ancestry, or most of them. He was dark, handsome, with blue eyes that were all melting cajolery one minute, and polar ice the next. On a dare he would do absolutely anything, no matter how risky; and if he loved chocolate more than liquor or marijuana, his fists were always ready to argue the point. Nobody, in all his fifteen years, had ever whipped Bobbie in a fair fight. He would have been what the old Irish of my girlhood called a "b'hoy."

I helped to raise him, at least for a while. His mother was my best friend. You know how a pretty girl usually pairs up with the other kind? Well, she was a lovely one—a gorgeous colleen. She married Tim Denellan, a good man, but no match for her in ambition. Bobbie was an only child.

I can still see him as a baby, sitting in his high chair, crying with impatience at dinnertime. He never cried otherwise. But if his mother dallied even for a moment after Bobby saw food, his face would screw up, and he would start to whimper. The portions he made away with were unbelievable. "Mo'!! Mo'!" he used to demand; until when finally satisfied, a merry smile touched his lips, and looking at you with those great, dancing blue eyes, he'd say gravely: "Aw done," and bang his spoon against the bowl.

"All done, are you?" Eileen would reply, feigning indignation. "About time, too!"

At three he was willful and imperious, and so attractive a child that the two of them were stopped every ten feet by adoring women. But he would do anything for those he loved, and at his most perverse always gave in either at the promise of chocolate in any form, or the threat of a friendly tickling. Just thrust a forefinger at his plump midsection, and he broke down, half delighted, half terrified that his sensitive ribs might be prodded.

We spoiled him dreadfully, I'm afraid. I have to plead guilty. I knew better! Spock and Gesell were my teachers. But Bobbie was too much for us. Nobody can love a child, and be so foolish about it, as an old maid.

Still, it might have worked out eventually, since Bobbie was really hard to spoil in any basic sense. But then fate took a hand; both the Denellans died in an auto accident, and Bobbie was an orphan at four. There were no available relations, so I tried to adopt him. How I tried! Talk about fighting City Hall; it's a wonder I wasn't deported altogether. But they couldn't give a male child to an unmarried woman of thirty-nine. For a while I was tempted to find a husband—any kind. I know now that wouldn't have been very easy. I was homely then, as I was even as a girl, and what man wants an ugly woman of middle age?

So they took Bobbie away to a foster home, and that's when he started to go bad. From there his path led inevitably to War Counselor of the Dukes, and then to a miserable, liquor-sodden death. I managed to see him fairly often, and he was pleasant to me for old times' sake. Thanks to him, I could do my work at all hours in perfect safety. The Dukes passed the word that old Miss Wallace was not to be harmed, and they were the law. That didn't mean anybody followed my advice, or that many brands were saved from the burning, but only that I was allowed to carry out my ineffective rituals as a well-meaning social worker.

I saw Bobbie for the last time three days ago. It was not a casual visit. I had received an anguished call from the mother of a girl named Mary Rio, one of the junior Princesses, and much cherished by them. I knew the child, she was only thirteen. Very lovely, even at that age; well developed physically, but not at all bright. Her mother was furious, spitting out her words in a way that suggested an enraged cat. It seems that Mary was pregnant—Mrs. Rio used much coarser language—and had named Bobbie as the boy responsible.

Of course, I knew what the woman wanted; there was only one way out according to her beliefs, even if the law sometimes sanctioned others. She expected me to force the children into a loveless, impracticable marriage. Just so the baby was born in wedlock, nothing else mattered to Mrs. Rio. Bobbie could be a pervert, unemployable, or insane, as long as he was Mary's legal husband in time. What a marriage that would be. A lovely, stupid child, and a bright, heedless angel of a boy.

I went to see Bobbie. He was polite as always, but I could tell he was laughing at me; there was a gay, electrical sparkle in those blue eyes. And God help me, when Bobbie looked at me like that, I could have hugged him to death if he'd just shot at the President.

"Relax, Aunt Betty," he told me. "That Rio chick knew exactly what she was doing. Like she was real hip. It was a rigged deal, just to hook me. Like all those Princesses, she's dying to get married. Not for this cat!"

"She's just a child," I reminded him. "Her mother is frantic."

"They'll get over it," he replied calmly. "I told Mary to take a trip to the country for a while. That's the cool way. I'll stand some of the cost—me and the Dukes."

"That might be best," I was forced to agree. I couldn't pretend that marriage was any solution, even if the courts would okay it at their ages. Fifteen and thirteen! Besides, I still hoped to see Bobbie aiming for a career in some professional field. He was more than intelligent enough.

"I hope there won't be any rumble over this," I said anxiously.

He grinned.

"Aunt Betty, after all these years you still don't dig the simple rules. Cats don't rumble with chicks. If the Princesses are mad at me, they'll just hen-talk me to death. Women! The only real gripe those gals have is that Mary saw me first. And let me tell you, she'll fight her own gang if they try to give me any trouble."

"Bobbie," I said gravely, "when are you going to clear out from all this and prepare for a real career?"

"Plenty of time," he smiled. "Right now I'm enjoying life. I can always become an eight-to-five working square."

He'd been saying that for three years now, with his grades dropping each semester, and this in a school with standards so low a baboon could easily make the honor roll. In another year he'd be an errand boy for some numbers racketeer; and after that the sky would be the limit unless he met the hangman along the road. It made me sick to think about it and be so helpless. I had no real influence over him, and his foster parents, God forgive them, never became close to the boy. Maybe I had a premonition—there's some Celt in me, too—because I grabbed and kissed him. He was surprised; I hadn't done that for years; but being basically a gentleman, didn't fight me; he just stiffened a little. Now he's dead.

I heard about it from Lieutenant Marer. He knows of my work in the area. It was a strange and sordid business. Late Friday night there had been a call from the Princesses' clubhouse. The girl who phoned was quite excited. She said that Bobbie Denellan had just died. Send a doctor, an ambulance—do something.

The ambulance crew found Bobbie stretched out on the big, gaudy divan, fully dressed except for his leather jacket. He was quite dead, and there was nothing to indicate the cause, although it seemed to be a heart case, since his face was flushed and damp, and his whole body contorted.

The girls, there were only eight there at the time, explained what had happened. They had been having a little party, as usual on Friday night, when just before dark, one of them saw Bobbie walking by, and suggested they invite him in.

Although rather surprised at such a cordial gesture on the part of Mary Rio's friends, he accepted the invitation. Once he was in, it had amused them to tease the boy into drinking. They knew, as all his friends did, that Bobbie didn't like liquor, and couldn't hold it. After taking several ounces of bourbon, he had passed out, and with much giggling they had put him on the divan to sleep it off, never expecting any more serious consequences. Then, suddenly, at about eleven at night, the sleeping boy began to thrash about, mumbling incoherently, his face pink and wet; and before they could even realize he was seriously ill, Bobbie stiffened and died. It was over in moments.

Naturally, the police insisted on an autopsy. It confirmed the girls' account. There was alcohol in Bobbie's blood, 0.26 percent, which means intoxication. His heart was full of blood, and had apparently stopped from shock of some sort. There was no sign of any physical cause other than the liquor. A husky fifteen-year-old was dead, it would seem, from a few ounces of alcohol. It was a puzzler, but there it was. They could slap a charge against the girls of drinking by minors, but to them that kind of trouble was routine. They knew that the juvenile authorities, up to their necks in muggings, rapes, and brutal assaults by mere children, wouldn't have much time for so minor a violation.

Not that I cared about that aspect myself. Bobbie was dead; that's all I could think of. There was nobody else in the world I loved. Emotionally, I was alone for good now. A barren woman of fifty, with the heart cut out of her work and life.

I had to talk to those girls. There must be something more they could tell me about the tragedy. They might be more frank with me than with the police. The situation just didn't make sense. Had the coroner slipped up? Violent deaths are not uncommon here; no wealthy people are involved; and a politician-doctor doesn't always do his best work in such circumstances. Maybe Bobbie had a weak heart. Or had been abusing himself with drugs. There had to be an explanation better than the official one. All my instincts told me so.

Last night I went to the clubhouse. I know most of the girls, of course. There were only a few there—six, to be exact. I looked for Mary Rio, but she wasn't one of them. According to the police, she hadn't been there the night Bobbie died, either.

Virginia was around, all right. She's the leader, and a tough one. We've had our clashes. She's a chunky blonde, not pretty, but with a lovely, white skin. The girls don't usually go in for violence, but the grapevine has it that Ginny once slashed a rival very badly, ruining her looks. The victim was a Deb, from across the river, and the act led to a near rumble.

I looked around at the hard young faces with their heavy enameling and false lashes. Always before I had fancied there was youthful innocence lost behind those unpleasant façades. This time, the illusion failed. Some of the other members might be salvaged, but this hard core seemed lost, damned forever. At least, that's how I felt with Bobbie's death filling my world.

"What's on your mind?" Virginia greeted me coolly, a cigarette in one red-nailed hand.

"It's about Bobbie," I told her. "I can't seem to make any sense out of the way he died. Isn't there anything you can tell me that the police don't know? I promise not to repeat a word."

That seemed to amuse them.

"Oh, we trust you, Miss Wallace," one of them said, with a snicker.

"Did he use dope, or anything? Or did he have a bad heart?"

"Yeah," Virginia said dryly. "He had a bad heart. Ask Mary Rio."

"You know I didn't mean that."

"Then what do you mean?" she said, her voice hard. "You accusing us of doping him?"

"Of course not. It was a natural death." I was lying then. *If they hadn't poured all that liquor into him, he'd be alive*, I thought.

"You bet it was. The cops said so. Not our fault if he couldn't hold a little bourbon, good stuff, too. Not rotgut."

"I didn't think Bobbie ever drank much," I said feebly, afraid to express my resentment more openly and risk getting no further crumbs of information, however grudgingly offered.

"He hated the stuff," Ginny said. "We had to make him plenty mad before he drank any."

"We told him he wasn't a man after all, just a little boy," Carmen Acosta said. "Oooh, that burned him. He said he'd show us. We had a drinking match."

"You shut up," Virginia said coldly.

"A drinking match?" I repeated.

"Sure; we matched him shot for shot."

"Only ours was tea," one of the girls volunteered, and the others giggled, only to stop suddenly as Ginny glared at them.

"Look," I begged shamelessly. "You're hiding something. Please tell me. I've got to know. You have my word—"

"Why not tell her?" the Kelly girl said, her sharp, pimply face twitching. "No witnesses down here—what can she prove? Our word against hers."

"Suppose she tips the Dukes?" someone shrilled.

"That'll be the day," Kelly jeered. "Old Wallace stirring up violence!"

I watched them, bewildered. There was a lot more behind this than I'd expected. Something dark and sinister. My expression brought screams of laughter from the girls. It was as heartless as the mewing of seagulls. They crowded closer, enjoying my distress.

"Will somebody please tell me what this is all about?" I demanded finally, making an effort to keep my voice firm and level.

"No!" Virginia snapped, her face deeply flushed. "Get out!"

"Tell her! Go on, tell the old creep!" some others yelled, and I could sense their leader wavering. The desire to shock and hurt was stronger than the almost instinctive caution.

Virginia's over-red lips tightened into a narrow, ugly gash.

"All right, I will." She stepped up to me, putting her brittle mask of a face only inches from mine. "We fixed your dear little Bobbie Denellan, but good. We taught him to mess around with a Princess and then chicken out on her. 'Go to the country,' he says. Well, he's in a nice, warm country now!" The others shrieked with laughter at this.

"I—I don't know what you mean," I quavered. "Was it the liquor? Did Mary …?"

"Leave her out of this; she had nothing to do with it. She's still mushy over him. It was us. Nobody can get a Princess into that kind of trouble and bug out. Duke or War Counselor or what!"

"Then what did happen that night? You must tell me—please."

"So tell her!" the girls shouted again; and their faces that should have seemed so young and fresh were ancient and malicious as they pressed closer.

"Sure, why not?" Virginia said coldly. "We knew that if we cut up that punk the way he deserved, the Dukes might give us a real bad time. It had to be done cool and quiet. Luckily we new all about Bobbie's big weaknesses—thanks to little Mary. Always talking about her boy, she was. We invited him down here just like we told the cops. No hard feelings, we said. What the hell, a girl of thirteen is old enough to know the score; if she gets into trouble, it's her own fault. We bugged him until he drank seven or eight good slugs of that stuff—it had a chocolate flavor—crazy! What do they call it again, Gail?"

"Cream of cocoa."

"That's it. He hated liquor, but with a chocolate flavor it was easier to convince him. When he passed out, we wrapped him in a blanket, with ropes on the outside, so only his head and feet stuck out at each end. Very careful; no marks on him. Oh, we played it cool. When he slept off some of the jag, we sobered him up with cold towels and things. Then we went to work on the punk."

I gaped at them uncomprehending. How could I match my mind with theirs?

"You raised him from a baby," Virginia reminded me contemptuously. "I'll bet that wasn't all just mother love. Why, you were gone on the kid—everybody could see that. And still she doesn't dig us. Let me give you a hint. We took off his shoes and socks."

"You devils!" I raged at them, still confused, groping for something dreadful just beyond my imagining. "What did you do to Bobbie?"

She waved something under my nose. Insolently she brushed my chin with it. A big quill feather. My stomach tightened, and I felt a surge of nausea. Suddenly I saw an unbearable vision. Oh, Bobbie, Bobbie—what a terrible way for you to die.

"We tickled him to death," Virginia hissed, her white face contorted. "The big idea—the great idea that leaves us clean. They can't pin a thing on the Princesses." She put one stubby hand on my shoulder, tightening its grip painfully. "Strong lad, your darling Bobbie. He almost tore that heavy wool blanket. Still, it was soon over; he didn't last more than an hour, did he girls?"

I don't remember how I got home. I only know that Bobbie is dead, and that I'm quitting. The devils; the murderous, giggling little devils.

Chain Smoker

If you want the pure, bracing air, the privacy, and the unspoiled coast of California Highway 1, there is, as with all good things, a price to be paid. But Rex Morland thought the price a cheap one. True, he had to drive thirty miles, round trip, to Seaview, the nearest town; and he couldn't get the electric company to bring him power; but the big tank of butane ten yards from his door kept not only a freezer and stove going, but also a fine brute of a generator. And since he made his living as a writer, his home was his office, where over the top of his typewriter he could see the thunderous surf battering the rocky shore ninety feet below.

Sometimes friends from Los Angeles or San Francisco, observing his isolation, and the steep, winding road that led from the highway to his house, itself quite hidden from above, would remark, "Isn't your wife afraid to live in such a lonely place? What if some criminal broke in at night, or something?"

Morland found this amusing. "It's the city jungles that are dangerous," he often reminded them. "Out here, there are nothing but raccoons, foxes, deer, and bobcats. Maybe a few rattlers, but no animal is as deadly as one of your big city delinquents, believe me!"

He honestly believed this himself; and it was true, in general; but what happens when evil from the city turns the isolation to its own advantage?

The ordeal began towards dusk of a fine August day. Morland's wife and his sixteen-year-old daughter, Kathy, were inside the house; he could hear them giggling over the dinner dishes, a sound that warmed his heart. He had gone out to take a reading on the big butane tank that kept the house livable. He knew he was childishly compulsive about this; the thing had been filled to capacity only six days earlier, but he had a foolish dread of finding himself without light, heat, or cooking facilities on some weekend, with the service company twenty-odd miles away, and closed until Monday. He also enjoyed checking; the serviceman had shown him how, and the operation fascinated him. You turned one indicator to the 100% mark, opened a valve, and then brought the first metal finger clockwise until the stream of escaping gas changed to a liquid spray. This evening it did so at the 73% mark, which meant that the tank was over three-quarters full. Not for the first time, his hand grazed the rushing flow of liquid and was badly stung; for the stuff, expanding as it blew free, became extremely cold. No doubt it could freeze a finger solid in a few seconds.

He gave a grunt of satisfaction to learn that so much of the gas remained, and stood up, turning towards the house. There was a stealthy footstep behind him; he whirled, startled, and almost bumped his nose on the gun muzzle. It was quickly withdrawn, however; the skinny youth who held it was taking no chance of its being grabbed.

"Who's inside?" the boy demanded in a hoarse whisper.

"Wha-what do you want?" Morland gulped, instead of answering him. "You can't be Kessler. He was picked up, at least—"

The boy laughed, a nickering sound without mirth. "Wanna bet? No hick sheriff can hold me."

"What happened?" Morland asked, not so much caring as playing for time. He had to get his bearings. The radio had reported earlier that Fred Kessler, psychopathic killer on the loose from Santa Cruz, had been captured near Seaview by a deputy sheriff.

"Since you ask so polite-like, I'll tell you," the boy said, still watching the lighted windows of the house. "I always carry a hide-out gun, where, I ain't telling. Nobody knows, because after I use it, they can't talk. The sheriff won't talk, either. I took his car, his gun, and even his cuffs, see?" He pulled them from his pocket with his free left hand, dangling them in front of Morland. "Then I headed south, towards San Luis; but I knew they'd get roadblocks up fast. So when I saw your box on the highway, I investigated. You're almost lost down here; can't even see the place from up there. I ditched the car in a gulley where they won't find it for days, and I'll stay with you folks for a while, until the fuzz gets tired of this stretch. They'll never figure I'm on foot, see? Now," his voice became urgent, almost savage, "who's inside there?"

"Just my wife and daughter."

"Dames, huh? Good; I can handle them."

"You can't stay here," Morland blurted, desperation in his cry.

"Wanna bet? If you all behave, nobody'll be hurt."

"How long?"

"How the hell do I know? You ask too many questions, Pop."

"But when you leave ..." Morland didn't dare press that point. He didn't have to.

"When I leave, you'll howl copper; sure. Only you won't, because I'll have one of them," he waved the gun muzzle towards the house, "with me. We've yakked enough," he added. "I could use some food, and this wind is chilly."

Resignedly, Morland took one step toward the house, but the boy blocked his path with a tigerish move, gun steady.

"Not you, Mac; I don't need you in there; I can handle them better alone. Three's too many to watch."

The heavy police revolver was pointing directly at Morland's chest, and for a moment he knew that the boy was ready to pull the trigger. Then the muzzle dropped, and Morland felt some of the ice leave his middle. He guessed the killer was afraid a shot might be heard; it was lucky he didn't realize how isolated this place really was. A cannon could go off here every five minutes and nobody would even notice it, especially with the surf beginning its evening thunder against the rocks below.

"What the hell," the boy muttered. "Might as well use these." He pulled out the cuffs again, peered at the butane tank, and snapped, "You were born lucky, Pop; some have it; some don't. Scrounge down by that pipe, quick like a bunny."

His pale eyes were glowing, and Morland knew it was no time to argue or delay. He crouched by the big cylinder, and held his tongue. The boy unlocked the cuffs, tossed them to Morland, and said, "One on that thick pipe, one on your wrist; I'm watching real close, and I know the right sound; I got reason to know."

Morland could believe that. It was getting quite dark now, but there was enough light from the house to make any fudging risky. He'd be no use to his family dead or with a cracked head; and a sick feeling in his stomach told him they might need help very badly soon. This punk had murdered five people in Santa Cruz, and had an earlier record involving crimes as unpleasant, if less permanent, in their effects on the victims. And Kathy was only sixteen, and too pretty; right now, Morland wished she were fat and raucous like her chum, Selma.

The cuffs clicked home; Kessler came close, gun ready, and checked them.

"Guess you'll stay put," he said, and turned toward the house. "Don't try any yelling," he added coldly. "It'll cost *them*."

Morland winced. This punk was good at the kind of psychology he needed in his business. Then he groaned as the front door opened, and Julie stood there,

"Rex," she called, "you're taking a long time with that tank. How can you even see in this light?"

In a few quick, feline bounds Kessler landed in front of her. "Inside," he ordered. "Quick like a bunny."

"Where's my husband?" Julie demanded, standing there like a rock.

"Do as he says!" Morland yelled. "I'm all right. Please, Julie, he means business. Do exactly as he says, and you'll be all right." He wished he could believe it himself; but in any case, it was the only thing to tell her.

She caught on quickly; Julie was always bright; and went into the house. The door closed behind her. By standing half upright in a terribly cramped position, Morland could watch through the living room window. Without wasting a moment, Kessler had zeroed in on the phone. Morland hoped he'd be dumb enough to tear it out, which might bring a repairman (*what good would that do?* he asked himself a second later) but the boy was too wise; he just sat near it, on the sofa.

By straining his ears over the surf, Morland could catch some of the conversation through the open windows. Kessler was demanding food, and the two women were getting some ready. Good, until he was fed, the danger was diminished; but Rex didn't like the way the boy was already watching Kathy; damn those toreador pants of hers—she ought to be wearing a flour-sack, a dirty, wrinkled, torn one.

It was time for action, not wishful thinking. He examined the cuffs, first by the feeble light reaching him from the house, and then, very cautiously, by the flame of his lighter. They were thick and heavy, but old fashioned, he guessed, from the look of them. He wasted fifteen minutes trying to pick the locks with odds and ends from his pockets, but old or not, they weren't that easy. Then he pounded metal with a variety of rocks, but didn't dare make too much noise. The rocks crumbled, but the steel only got shiny where it was battered.

He rose and watched the house again. They were serving the food now, and the boy seemed almost as anxious to smoke as to eat. Clearly, he had been starved for cigarettes, and was something of a chain smoker.

"You dames can cook, all right," Morland heard him say, as he wolfed the warmed-over roast lamb of their dinner. "Kathy won't have no trouble getting a man, not a bit. Good cook, and good looks; not every broad can wear them pants," he added, eyes smoldering.

Morland didn't like the trend of that conversation one little bit. He had to get free; get help; do something; had to. Once that killer was full of food, he'd be ripe for mischief, and Morland was afraid; more scared than ever in his life before, and not for himself.

He yanked at the cuffs in a frenzy that was nearly hysterical, and regained control by a concentrated effort of will. *Use your brains!* he told himself; *don't panic, not now. Use that writer's imagination, if you ever did believe in it.*

All right; I'm calm now. What can I do; what have I got to work with? Nothing in my pockets; I've tried that angle. And I can't move very far tied to this tank. He tensed then. *The tank! Surely there was an angle. What angle? Fire!* He could open the main valve, use his lighter, send a column of flame up. His elation died. *Idiot!* Before any help came, Julie and Catherine might be dead. And even if Kessler panicked and ran, leaving them unharmed, this whole hill would catch fire; the house would go; the flames would surge through the dry bush; the women might not make it to the highway even if they didn't stop for him, which they would; imagine Julie and Kathy leaving him to burn! If only the cuffs were off, then there were really angles. They wouldn't burn off, not without ruining his hands, too.

Suddenly he remembered the cold rush of liquefying gas. Cold was useful, too. It made metal brittle; he'd used that gimmick in a story once. What an idiot not to think of it sooner, now that it counted.

Hastily he fumbled with the small valve, opening it wide, and turning the indicator until the stream was at its chilliest. Then he directed the flow against the middle of the cuffs, watching the steel grow a coating of frost. He let the process continue for several minutes, then shut off the gas, and used all his strength to bring leverage against the frozen metal by wedging the cuffs between the heavy pipe and the side of the tank. With modern steel it might not have worked; with this, success came with almost ridiculous ease. The metal snapped, and he was free.

Morland sprang to his feet, swaying a little from the pull of cramped muscles. He approached the house very cautiously, careful not to break a single twig. What he saw through the window almost drove him wild with fury. Kessler had Kathy on his lap. Julie, her face grey and years older, watched in helpless horror. As for the girl, she seemed like an automaton worked by wires.

There was an axe among the garden tools. In three strides Morland reached and seized the thing. He'd crash in there and chop the punk to bits; he'd splatter him all over the room; he'd—damned if he would! It was crazy, foolish stuff again. The boy would shoot him dead, and that would be the end for all of them. No; instead lure Kessler out here. But he wouldn't come; Morland knew that. The boy would merely say, "Come in with your hands up, or I'll fix the women," or words to that effect. And Morland would have no choice. That still wasn't the answer. He had to get him outside without making him suspicious. But how?

Then he had it. The generator. Shut that off, and the lights would go out. Kessler would ask the women, find out about the generator in its little shack, and come out to fix it. Then Morland would be waiting with the axe.

Hurriedly, he went to the shack, but once there, he hesitated, trying to figure all the angles. Would it be better to go up to the highway for help? There wasn't time; it would take ten minutes to get there, and traffic was light on a weeknight. Lord knows how soon he'd find help; and the women would still be hostages. No, this was the only way.

It was the work of moments to pull the cut-off switch and stop the full-throated hum of the generator. The lights grew dim in the house, then died out. Morland, axe in hand, waited at the locked door.

He heard Kessler questioning the women. Then the boy said, "I don't like this; I smell trouble. Know what? I think your daddy got loose, Kathy, honey. He'd like to sucker me out there in the dark. But I ain't no sucker; people are learning that. I want a flashlight; gonna do me some shooting."

The women were reluctant to help him, but after Kathy gave a little squeal of pain, Mrs. Morland knew it was hopeless, and gave Kessler what he wanted. The boy locked them in the windowless dressing room, and flash in hand, came to the side door. This was bad; Morland knew he couldn't lay for Kessler there; he would be seen first, and shot. The whole plan was coming apart at the seams.

Quickly, his brain feverishly active, Morland scuttled back to the generator house. But the way Kessler was waving that flash, it was impossible to ambush him. He came along, all too cautiously, quite sure of himself, even puffing a cigarette. Morland had no doubt the boy could use that gun; the way he held it was a clear indication of that.

Morland played for time. He grabbed a rock and flipped it far to the left of Kessler. The flash flickered that way, and the killer drifted over for a look. That gave Morland a chance to get to the butane tank. With a few quick twists he shut off the main valve on top; no gas could get to the generator now. Then, before Kessler got near the shack, Morland ducked in and opened the gas valve of the generator. Nothing came out, of course, the main valve being closed. Just in time, he slipped out and returned to the tank, crouching behind it in the dark.

Kessler warily entered the shack, put the flash on a shelf so that it lit up the generator, and prepared to get the thing going again. From his place by the tank Morland could see Kessler locate the switch and jiggle it. Now was the moment, as the boy bent close to the generator, puzzled by the lack of response to the switch, cigarette end glowing as he puffed nervously.

Morland opened the tank's master valve wide. There was a hissing roar in the little shack as butane surged from the generator's open petcock; and almost simultaneously a whoomp of igniting gas as the flammable stuff, pouring out in heavy concentration encountered the glowing cigarette. The screaming was a sort of anticlimax.

By shutting off the main valve in a hurry, and the use of a fire extinguisher from the house, Morland managed to save most of the shack, as well as the generator. There was little he could do for Kessler, although he honestly tried. After he had comforted the two women, who were verging on hysteria, he ventured on a feeble joke.

"Damn it, we'll be out of butane again, and the thing was just filled!"

Swan Song

All criminals are warped to some extent, but none suffered from a stranger aberration than Sampson Theodore Pardoe, known—although never to his face—as "Singin' Sam." In his youth, thanks to overhasty screening of numerous applicants, he had briefly wangled a place in the high school chorus. The director, a simple, gentle soul, assuming that a waggish student had smuggled a cat into the ranks—what else could account for such discordant, mewling sounds?—investigated, and found a fat, sullen kid who obviously couldn't carry a tune three bars if it had handles. Pardoe was promptly evicted, and two days later the teacher got a bad beating from five boys wearing false faces.

Later, as he worked his way bloodily to the top of an illegal empire, Sam, still self-deluded, and daily less likely to be undeceived, took lessons from the best musicians in the state, including a number of opera and concert stars. None of these, after looking into his shallow eyes, hard and shiny as greased marbles, cared to tell him that more mellow sounds were produced nightly, with less effort, by the coyotes in the hills. Instead, they accepted his generous fees and implied, without saying as much, that he was truly gifted as a tenor.

Since the biggest lies are most easily swallowed when fed to oneself, Pardoe honestly believed his voice a match for that of Bjoerling, McCormack, or even Caruso.

Since he controlled all the juke boxes in the state, it was easy for him to push his own records, pressed under the "Aristocrat" label. And so many a teenager, relaxing in a malt shop, choked suddenly over his sticky concoction at hearing between the pelvic mooing of his own favorites, a thin, reedy tenor, horribly off-key and quavering as if the singer faced imminent execution, bleating out some sentimental ballad like "Mother Machree" or "The Bluebird of Happiness." For Pardoe, like certain Nazi officials, managed to combine an excess of mawkishness with the feral behavior of a jungle beast.

Sam also fancied himself a composer, and had turned out dozens of songs, all so sugary they could send a diabetic into a coma at fifty feet.

To be sure, few people ever played a record of "Pardoe the Great" voluntarily, except for laughs; but the owners of bars or restaurants found it advisable to feed the juke box from their registers. If they neglected that precaution, a checker, tanned, sharply dressed, and with eyes like two ice-caverns on some frozen, uninhabited planet, was certain to call and inquire just what the fellow had against Aristocrat Records and its top star.

If the answer was unsatisfactory—and a checker is hard to please— another visitor, seldom under seven feet in height and two hundred plus pounds in weight, most of it muscle, acted as a kind of human teaching machine—one programmed in advance by no gentle soul.

It was also rumored, and later proved true, that Pardoe carried his obsession even further. Whenever he decreed the elimination of anybody, the condemned man was given a special send-off; a solo by the boss himself. A few hardy wights, aware that for once they had nothing to lose, spoiled the occasion by laughing.

Nor was that the whole story, either. Sam itched to create, seldom missing a chance, and if the victim was important, extra honors were quite in order. In that case, Pardoe might even write a song in his honor, for he studied composition, too, and from a student of Bartok's at that.

And so Singin' Sam Pardoe had made his mark in the world, and if this brief account of his habits seems at all funny, the humor belongs in the same category as those practical jokes that are so amusing to read about only because they've been played on somebody else. There was no fun in the situation for those who paid protection money, or for men beaten to whimpering pulps, or for those unfortunates who died to the sound of amateurish singing.

But Pardoe made a bad mistake when he ordered the kidnapping of Kathy, and met my uncle, Charles Roussel, head-on, so to speak. And it's at this point that I came into the matter, and can speak out of my own knowledge from now on.

Uncle Charles sent for me on June 8th, and I dropped everything to come. For one thing, he had paid for my education as an electronics engineer, and for another, it was never easy to say no to him. People who knew about the man only from the press, thought of him as a playboy, because of the money he inherited. They forgot his fine war record, the many distant places he had explored; the tigers he had killed—on foot, and even after dark—and his exploits under water. Something else that Pardoe didn't know, as well as the world in general, was that my uncle's mother was descended from one of Cortés' officers—a collection of the toughest and most ruthless fighting men that ever terrorized a whole continent against numerical odds so great the facts about the expedition would be unbelievable as mere fiction; only historical records can be convincing in the matter. You had only to watch Roussel and hear his voice, like something of bronze, to realize the enormous presence of the man. He has a granitic head, with glowing, deep-socketed, hypnotic eyes, and moves like a trained dancer—the Russian kind that leaps into the air as if propelled by hidden springs, and then comes down—how is it done?—like a drifting feather. Even his ears have significance; I've seen them, so help me, appear pricked and pointed at just those times when a wolf's might be. No doubt it was only my imagination, but since I don't ordinarily have one, its mushroom growth in the circumstances has evidential value in itself.

This is inadequate, but explains why I'd have come even if I owed him nothing.

When I saw him, in that huge study that looks like something out of a high-budget movie, he was fingering a slip of paper which had cost him more than fifty thousand dollars and almost two years of relentless investigation.

"I'll need the Chief," he told me, his fierce, craggy face showing only a small part of what he felt. "Monty, too; I must have him. Then we'd better get O'Doul; he knows the breed inside out, and can handle a lie detector. It wouldn't do for me to make a mistake. I want the right man badly—but only the right man. No chance to do it legally in this fool country, so it's the old *lex talionis* for us. Two years," he added, almost in a whisper. "The rocks I had to pry up to reach the crawlers underneath. But the worst of them aren't like this Pardoe swine"—jabbing the paper with a lean finger. For a moment, then, he stood there, blind-eyed, before stabbing me with an imperious gaze.

"There's a special job for you: an electronics gadget I'll need, but you should be in on the kill in any case. After all, you were Kathy's favorite." I saw him swallow hard, but his face showed no change of expression. No father ever loved a child more than Charles Roussel loved his daughter, the wispy, quicksilver, gentle little girl of eight—now dead, with grave unknown.

"Well," my uncle snapped. "You heard what I want. The Chief should be at his Lodge in Maine. Have him fly here at once. You'll be able to contact Monty at the R.A.F. Club in London; I hope to hell he's not off to Timbuctoo or Iraq as usual, but run him down anyhow. I'll scare up O'Doul myself; had a card last week."

I didn't know exactly what he was up to, but could have made a good guess that somebody named Pardoe would soon be having a bad time. I must have groaned a little, not being very happy with the extra-legal capers of Roussel & Company; my own life is strictly pasteurized in that sense, and I hoped to keep it so. Nevertheless, when my uncle gave an order in that tone of voice, somebody jumped—in this case, me.

You might wonder at his self-assurance—all right, arrogance—in expecting a group of his friends to abandon their present concerns and assemble at his command, coming from the far reaches of the world on short notice. But they were a loyal bunch, with ties that bound them closer than most brothers.

Take the Chief—almost pure Apache stock—who had trained my uncle in woodcraft. He could not only catch a weasel asleep, but steal the little killer's nightcap if it wore one.

Then there was Monty, immaculate, horse-faced, with that perfect English grooming that made him look fresh from a night's sleep and a cold bath whether you met him in the Queen's box at some sweepstakes or in a nomad's tent on the Gobi Desert. Montague Travers, V.C., D.S.O.—explorer, commando, and gentleman, up to a point. Few knew it, but he'd also taken a Double First in Literature at Oxford, and was the author, under an assumed name, of a monograph on the poetry of Donne. The experts liked it, too.

Lastly, O'Doul. You'd expect him to be called Patrick or Terence, but his mother was Italian, and had christened him Cesare, which most people mispronounced. He had been, among other things, a Captain of Detectives in Chicago, an expert with the lie detector, and one of the best combat sergeants in Korea.

All four men were pirates, but of a special kind. The true, historical ones were a bloody, cruel, and treacherous lot, possessing only one virtue—courage. My uncle and his three henchmen had much more than that: integrity and a code that, while elastic at times, was considerate of the weak and helpless. A human life to them was nothing sacred *per se*. They risked their own hides freely in any cause that appealed to them enough; so why should they overvalue the continued existence of a dope-peddler, vice-king, or blackmailer? If they were too quick about taking the law into their own hands, it was also true that in some countries the grasp of justice is feeble.

But whatever—or wherever—they were, all three came at my uncle's summons. It was quite a collection. Chief Dobie was small, swarthy, and tense, with a time-clawed face blank as the back of a shovel. He never smiled. Monty liked to play the traditional dim-witted toff, putting in "old boys" and even "Don't-chu knows" in an affected drawl, particularly when matters reached a crisis. The slower his voice, I'd learned, the quicker his reactions.

O'Doul was less of an individual than the others, at least outwardly. He was slender, wiry, redheaded, and had the most electric-blue eyes in the world. They twinkled a lot; and in fact his whole aspect was so good-humored that he made a perfect decoy on the Bunco Squad—a swindler felt sure this happy clown would fall for anything. Yet, of all four men, he was perhaps the most shrewd, with a deep understanding of psychology.

"I'll make this short," Uncle Charles told us, when we were assembled in the study. "You know what happened two years ago. Somebody kidnapped Kathy out of her bed, and set the ransom at fifty thousand dollars. I paid it, following instructions to the letter, but she was never returned. I didn't mind so much being taken for the money. I can understand some crook's wanting a piece of my inheritance, and playing rough to get it. We've been on the wrong side of the law ourselves a few times. But there was no excuse for not returning the girl. I know she's dead; my wife knew it too; and that's what killed her.

"I want the man behind that operation—want him so badly it's a red-hot lump in my guts." He held up that slip of paper. "Now I've got his name: 'Sampson T. Pardoe.' " His voice was level, but there was a purring undertone in it that made my neck hairs tingle. "Know him, Cesare?"

"You've got a bad one—and big. He's moved up fast. It won't be any cinch, getting at Pardoe."

"Good!" my uncle said. "More for him to lose."

He didn't ask Monty or the Chief. Monty knew a lot of English crooks; some of them, I'm sorry to say, were his friends. The reckless rogues—the kind that took all the money from the train—millions of pounds; years back—and fought society in a half-honorable way, without hurting the weak or foolish. But Monty wouldn't know Pardoe's kind. And Dobie was more likely to have information about a "bad" bear or wolverine than a city mobster.

But they all had loved Kathy, both for her sunny moods, which were commonest; and those sudden somber unplumbed silences that make children so wonderful and mysterious.

"He has a tough hold," O'Doul said, "and a rough lot of helpers."

"But not like mine," Uncle Charles said, naked pride in his voice. "Well, here's what I have on Pardoe. The man who sold it to me didn't take any chances; he's left for South America. I only hope," he gritted, "that he falls into that piranha pool. You remember the one, Monty—where that wounded jaguar was skeletonized in a few minutes. He's safe from me; that was the deal, and he's only a jackal; but still he had a hand in the filthy business ..."

He then gave most of the facts I've detailed at the beginning of this account.

"Pardoe has an estate near Silver Beach. We'll do a recon, although I'm pretty sure of the layout. There are three guards, I'm told. No matter what, we take the guy, and bring him here. No use being legal. It's *lex talionis* again. I'll need your lie detector," he told O'Doul. "To make sure he's guilty—not that I doubt it—and to find out where they … where Kathy is. Jim," he added, looking at me, "can skip the recon; he'll be building an electronics gadget for me."

I wanted to object; the whole business was near criminal and very risky; and I didn't like the implications of my own job. I wasn't quite clear on how the device would be used, but had some unpleasant suspicions. Uncle Charles had blandly avoided telling me just what he intended it for. But with his cold gaze on me, I just gulped and said nothing. If I ended up in prison, it was no more than I owed him.

When we left the study, I turned to Monty, who seemed most likely to know, and asked: "What's this '*lex talionis*' bit? I don't get the reference."

"Revenge, Old Testament style," he said crisply, his face hard. "Eye for an eye. Can't blame Charles when I think of little Kathy. What if that pig sang to her before …?" Then, as if his own words couldn't carry the sheer weight of his emotion, he quoted, in a voice like Gielgud's:

> *"Does thy soul*
> *Not wear a fleshy shirt, a cloak of skin,*
> *Art not sewn up with veins and pegged together*
> *With bony sticks and hinges?*
> *If thou hast a life*
> *And keep'st it in the cupboard of thy body,*
> *In the least corner, the minutest pore,*
> *More secret than the sunshine in a flint,*
> *I'll drag it out and cast it for a sop*
> *To the three-gated throat of Pluto's hound.*
> *So shut your soul's door closed and come on!*
> *Wert thou like the air, the water or the fire,*
> *Invulnerable though pierced,*
> *I'd quench thee, dam thee*
> *Or breathe thee up."*

I assumed that the savage lines, so charged with hate, were Donne's, but learned much later they came from Beddoes.

"Sorry," Monty said immediately. "The thing just popped into my head, and I slung it off towards Pardoe. A sort of pledge, old boy," he added, shifting to his drawl, "of what's coming to the swine."

"As a hot-blooded Italian Celt," O'Doul said dryly, "let me call your attention, Chief, to a typical chilly Englishman."

Dobie grunted. His vocabulary seemed to consist of about a dozen brief guttural sounds; to a casual listener they were all alike, but his intimates recognized the subtle nuances. In this case, the grunt said plainly: "Too much paleface jabber; I don't get it."

The preliminaries took several days. By that time I'd built the gadget my uncle wanted, which involved a sensitive mike and a weird electromagnetic complex. Then there was a final council of war, during which they collated their information and made a tactical plan.

"All right," Uncle Charles said. "This is the deal. There are two guards outside, and one in the house. The servants will be in their own quarters, well out of earshot. Pardoe's wife left him years ago; he has no kids; and his current mistress is doing a show in Vegas. To get back to the goons, they're Tommy Gentz, Wally Lopez, and 'Big Louie' Dean. What'd you get on them from the cops, Cesare?"

"I found out quite a bit. Rough boys, all of 'em. Records miles long, but hardly ever taken any big raps; too much money and influence behind 'em. Let me see." He ticked off the items on his fingers. "Gentz: assault with a deadly weapon more than once. Muggings; used to beat up storeowners so they'd put in pinball machines. Never actually killed anybody, as far as I know. Wally Lopez is a knife man. He got away with at least two murders for Pardoe. He can throw it, too, like a carny pro, so be careful. Big Louie is garbage. Dope peddler, rapist, child molester. But a nasty fighter close in: bites, gouges, and uses his nails. Vermin!"

"Fine," my uncle said. "I see we needn't be gentle with that gang. Don't plan on killing 'em, but if Big Louie gives you any trouble at all, don't hesitate to finish him off. Even if we're after a tiger, it won't hurt to step on a roach."

My part in the operation, as it turned out, was largely that of a spectator. Uncle Charles knew that I don't have his buccaneer flair, and to be fair, didn't want me too deeply involved. It was morally wrong—the whole deal—and I might have begged off, but remembering Kathy and the solemn way she used to line up her dolls for obscure lectures, I didn't want to stand aloof.

"We'll leave at eleven," was the final word. "Any questions?"

There were none. The four men had worked together before. Chief Dobie, his wrinkled face wooden, drew out a knife so that the light caught its blade in a sinister wink of polished steel. I never did know where he stashed it, the thing seemed to leap from nowhere into his hand. He claimed—but only when drunk—that the weapon had once belonged to Cochise. Since he didn't talk while sober, I had my doubts; Dobie did tend to play up his Apache origins. As to this gesture, I must confess that any affection he'd had for Kathy was well concealed, and he might have merely indicated a desire to cut somebody for my uncle's sake. But Indians, while not emotional with whites, are said to show plenty of warmth towards their own families, so I may be unjust, and he may have loved Kathy, too.

Monty just said musingly: "Should be a good show."

And O'Doul patted the case containing his sophisticated, much-miniaturized polygraph, and said: "The Iron Maiden's ready."

We talk glibly about "eternal vigilance," but there's no such thing. Even a cat at a mousehole must shift its attention now and then. Guards tend to become careless when nothing happens after weeks or months. Pardoe's men were no exception. After all, they probably figured, what's the danger? Only a madman or fool would dream of attacking a man as powerful and ruthless as their boss. To the public, he was now legitimate: construction work, juke boxes, Member of the Board, Friend of Underprivileged Children—all the usual camouflage that works so well in our strange society.

The two outside guards—Gentz and Lopez—had about a square block to control. The estate was on a bluff, so the sea was a sentry; there was an electrified fence, too.

But to an ex-commando like Monty, that was no problem. Using insulated wire cutters, and some "cheaters" that kept the circuit unbroken, he soon made a gap we could crawl through.

At a word from Roussel, Monty and the Chief slipped away like ghosts—except that we all wore black, and had nylons over our faces—to stalk the two guards. The three of us then waited fifteen minutes; there was a faint hiss, and the Englishman reappeared. In the moonlight we could see a bloody groove on the side of his neck.

He touched it, smiled tightly, and said: "Lopez. Fast boy with a knife; he had a new kind of hold, I think; almost worked."

"Dead?" my uncle asked.

"Broke his arm. He's well hog-tied."

Another five minutes went by with broken-backed slowness, then the Chief returned, rising silently from the brush, so that I jumped.

"Get him?" Uncle Charles demanded, more for the record than because he had any doubts.

Dobie grunted in a tone that meant yes.

"Have to kill him?"

Another grunt; this one said no.

"Soon he die," the Chief added, becoming garrulous.

"Fine," my uncle said. "That leaves Big Louie in the house. He'll be close to Pardoe, so watch out. I think," he said quietly, "I'd like to tackle him myself, unless something interferes. All right, let's move in."

He led the way to the building. We'd managed to get a plan from the Hall of Records, and knew the layout. One window was lit up. "Pardoe's study," Monty said. "He's there right now."

We cut a pane from a side window, and after opening it, climbed in. I helped O'Doul with the case. I was the only one who made any noise going through; the others might have been tiptoeing on mattresses.

We found ourselves in a large room, apparently devoted to music, since there was an enormous Bechstein piano there. My uncle crept to the door, opened it a crack, and peered into a dimly lighted hall. It seemed a mile long, and was luxuriously carpeted in rose-color.

The five of us padded down the corridor, Uncle Charles in the lead. We had almost reached the end of it, when I scraped one shoe against a small stand holding a vase of flowers. The noise seemed incredibly loud somehow. We all froze, and for a moment thought nobody had heard us. Then a door just opposite was flung open to disgorge a huge, swag-bellied man, seemingly berserk.

He was about to yell; I could see, in that slow-motion fashion typical of one's perceptions, so nightmare like, at critical moments, his blubbery lips beginning to part. They were very red.

But my uncle, gliding in on the giant with a kind of ballet pirouette, it was so graceful and swift, ducked under the man's clutching fingers and struck a single blow at the front of his throat. It seemed a mere flick of the hand, delivered with the edge of the palm, but it must have crushed Big Louie's larynx, because he struggled for breath, wheezing horribly, his face turning blue as he pawed at his neck.

With scarcely a pause, Charles brought his foot up from the floor in a savage kick—a trick learned from a French master of the *savate*—and buried it in Louie's overhanging midsection. It sounded like a mighty blow on a wet drum. The hood doubled over, retching, and my uncle with a mirthless grin gave him the coup de grâce—a side-fisted wallop just behind the ear that would have stunned a bull. It did more; Big Louie was dead almost before he hit the carpet. He would molest no more children.

"We'll lug his late gutship back where he came from," Uncle Charles said in a low voice. "Just in case some nosy servant comes by, although they should all be bedded down by now."

Monty and I took care of that, and the way was clear to the study. Luckily, it had huge doors of solid oak, which were tightly shut, so that nothing short of a dynamite explosion could have been heard inside the room.

Pardoe was surprised when we crashed in, but took it coolly—at first. He was a smallish man, very neat, with fluffy hair so light it looked platinum blond; he was deeply tanned, having just returned from Florida.

His hand was flying towards a desk drawer, but Monty's big Webley was out, and Pardoe had sense enough to freeze. He'd have been wiser to take the slug.

Ignoring the man's furious questions and sadistic threats, the Chief and O'Doul tied him to the armchair with straps they had brought.

"Don't waste any time hoping for your goons," my uncle advised him. "Two are dead and the other one out of action."

"What is this?" Pardoe demanded, regaining control of himself. "You can't be legit, not with this operation."

"I'm Charles Roussel," my uncle said. "Kathy's father." Pardoe blinked, and the color left his face. "These others can stay nameless, since they're here for me."

"Make some sense, will you? I never heard of a Kathy."

"Or of me, I suppose," Uncle Charles said dryly. "All set?" he asked O'Doul.

The detective, who had been assembling his polygraph, said: "Any time, Charles."

"We're going to ask you a few questions now," my uncle said to Pardoe. "I think you know why. I mean the kidnapping and murder of my little girl two years ago."

"I'm not answering any questions!" Pardoe snapped. "I don't know a thing about that job. I'm a legitimate businessman."

"We'll see. I advise you to cooperate," Roussel said, that purr sounding in his voice again. I seemed to see a black leopard, its lips drawn back over white fangs.

"It's illegal. When I tell the Commissioner—"

"Very funny. You jokers who flout the law should remember that others may be just as uninhibited, and in a better cause." He looked at O'Doul. "Hook him up."

With deft fingers, the detective attached blood-pressure cuffs, the skin electrodes, and other sensory devices that made up his intricate machine. His work done, he looked at Charles, who nodded.

"A few routine ones to calibrate with," Cesare said. "Is your name Sampson T. Pardoe? Answer yes or no—nothing else."

"Go to hell. I got nothing to say."

My uncle's deep-set eyes, full of fire, rested on him.

"Chief!"

Dobie slouched forward, the knife leaping into his hand. I could smell him—a wild-animal odor overlaid with woodsmoke, stale grease, musk, and the faint reek of many a weird feast, because in the field he ate snakes, insects, porcupines, lizards, and anything else available. The blade licked out, and Pardoe gave a little cry. A red line on one cheek was oozing blood.

"Is your name Sampson T. Pardoe?" O'Doul asked again, a cheerful Celtic lilt in his voice.

"—you! I don't scare."

"If he doesn't answer in ten seconds," Uncle Charles said, "put out his left eye."

The knife point neared Pardoe's face. He looked at Dobie, whose eyes are like wet licorice drops for all the expression they show. The Chief's horny thumb pinned the man's lid …

"Yes! All right; I'm answering. I'm Pardoe, damn you!"

Calmly, then, O'Doul asked more questions along the same lines: place of birth; address; age; weight—and studied the lines squirming out on his charts. After that, with a glance at Roussel, he began the serious work.

"Do you remember a girl named Kathy?"

"No—that is, I read about the snatch."

"Did you mastermind it?"

"No."

"He's lying," Cesare said, and Pardoe's face was wet.

"Is the girl dead?"

"I don't know, I tell you."

"Chief!" my uncle said, his voice gritty.

"Okay, okay; she's dead; but I didn't want that. It was Big Louie— he crossed me."

O'Doul peered at a slip of paper.

"This note says: 'We've got the dough; it was easy. Now have Louie get rid of the girl. But first, bring her to me.' "

From several feet away, I could see the recording pen jump making a huge squiggle on the chart. Of course, it wasn't the original note; that had been destroyed promptly; but Uncle Charles had learned the gist of it from his informer, and the paraphrase was close enough to jar Pardoe, obviously.

"No—I swear I didn't. I wanted to send her back. She was a nice little kid. I wouldn't hurt her."

"He's lying again," the detective said coldly.

"No! The machine's wrong. It was Louie."

"Now," my uncle said, almost to himself, "I have to know where."

"Can do," Cesare said. "Just a matter of time. And this map." He unfolded it in front of Pardoe's wild eyes. "Was she killed in this north part?"

"I don't know. No!"

"West?"

"No."

"He's lying; it was west, all right. She buried there?"

"No."

"Hmph," O'Doul muttered. "That's true, apparently. But then—wait a minute; I get it. Dock area."

From then on, it was easy. Kathy had been killed by Big Louie at Pardoe's orders. He had never intended to return her. She was too bright, and could identify him. After talking to the girl, and realizing that she hadn't learned to fear, only to love, and saw the world with clearer eyes than most adults, Pardoe had winced at the thought of Kathy on the witness chair against him.

That was bad enough, but somehow, although none of the questions was directed to that end, we guessed that she had laughed at his singing—merrily, and without malice, but with all the precocious musical knowledge of a child who played English madrigals and Mozart on her own phonograph. She actually must have believed, the darling innocent, that Pardoe was trying to amuse her.

My uncle drew a hissing breath at the inference—that Kathy had died partly because she giggled at Pardoe's singing.

The relentless inquiry went on until we learned where the girl's body had been dropped at sea.

"I'll get a diver," Uncle Charles said dully. "At least, I can put Kathy by her mother. And now," he added, his voice hardening, "it's time to take this animal back with us."

He didn't ask for details of Kathy's death, which was wise. It was easier to hope that the end had been relatively swift and merciful, that her shining spirit had gone out of this world gently, gently.

All of us felt the same way; if Pardoe had tried to tell us, we would have stopped his mouth.

They hustled Pardoe out of the house, over the silent grounds of the estate, and through the gap in the fence to the station wagon parked a few hundred feet away. The Chief's knife was never far from the captive's throat, and he had orders to use it if the man made a sound.

Back at my uncle's place, which was even bigger and more isolated than Pardoe's, they led him to the room Roussel had prepared—with me as a reluctant assistant. It was just a concrete shed, once used for storage, about twelve feet square, and tall enough for a man to stand up in without bumping his head. For furniture there was a wooden chair, a small table with a five-pound package of biscuits on it, and incongruously enough, a water cooler, complete with paper cups.

Pardoe, sweating and tense, was placed in the chair, and my uncle pulled a heavy chain tightly around his waist, secured it with a padlock, and carried the other end to a thick, steel ring set deep into the wall, where he fastened it with another lock.

At the far end of the shed, where Pardoe couldn't get at it, was a large glass bottle with a wide mouth. It was full of acid. Suspended over it was the electromagnet leading to the gadget I'd built.

"In this state," Uncle Charles told Pardoe, "killers die in the gas chamber. I don't go in for torture," he added grimly, "but you can end yours whenever you like. Hand him the microphone," he told me.

I held it out to Pardoe, who looked at it blankly, eyes rolling in his head, and then took it as if the thing were a cobra.

"In one minute after leaving here," my uncle said, "I'll pull a switch. If you're singing by then, the current will keep flowing to the magnet. Give me the pellets," he told Monty, and was handed two white "eggs" of cyanide, each with an iron pin through it. Uncle Charles stepped to the magnet, held the heads of the pins against it, and left the deadly little globes hanging there.

"As long as you sing, they'll stay put. The minute you stop for— how long, Jim?" The question was shot at me.

"If he starts again in thirty seconds, they won't fall," I explained, feeling slightly ill. It hadn't been easy to arrange that set-up. In fact, none of the contraption's parts was a cinch to design. The difference between noise and melody is one of regularity and periodicity in the sound waves. Mere talking or clatter wouldn't keep the electricity going—only the semblance of a tune, even a shaky one typical of Pardoe.

"My throat!" Pardoe husked. "It's too dry!—I can't sing. Don't pull the switch—please. I'll pay anything; I got money. I'll leave the country—"

"There's water," my uncle said, his face more granitic than ever. "Food, too. I don't know how long you can last before your vocal cords swell up, but you can quit any time; it's up to you. Better start now; we're leaving."

"No!" Pardoe begged, jumping up and throwing his full weight against the chain. "Don't—please—my God, you can't!"

"Sing," Roussel said. "Or die. I don't care which. Just a matter of time, anyhow."

"I can't think of anything," Pardoe sobbed. "I forget the words, honest to God." He was on his knees. Dobie grunted in disgust; Monty walked out; and O'Doul swore softly.

"Uncle Charlie—" I began, but he cut me off with an impatient wave of his hand.

"Try the song you used on Kathy," he said. Then, as if the words were choking him, which might have been the case: "I was told … by one of your own men … that you sang … 'I'll Take You Home Again, Kathleen' … to her … before handing my Kathy over to … Big Louie."

His jaw muscles stood out in knotted cords as he spoke; his hands were clenched into bloodless fists; and he rocked drunkenly on his feet. I'd never seen him in such a state, and feared it might be a stroke. Then, without saying another word, he went through the doorway, and we followed him. Pardoe was pleading incoherently as my uncle shut the door, muffling the sounds. He had tacked rubber strips around the edges to seal the shed.

I didn't stay for the end, not having a strong enough stomach. But the four of them played stud poker on a folding table set up just within earshot, using a lamp at night. I doubt if their performance at the game was up to par. I learned later that Pardoe lasted fifty-three hours and nineteen minutes—probably drinking a lot of water—before his voice gave out and the pellets dropped, filling the room with cyanide gas.

But, to me, the really chilling part was this. Because he was too terrified to think clearly, and had only my uncle's bitter remark to guide him, Pardoe actually stuck to a single line of the song, repeating it all that time until his throat clogged. I can't imagine how Uncle Charlie could stand it; surely, in the circumstances, he was being punished as much as Pardoe. Hearing it just once was too much for me; that's when I ran.

To this day I can't forget the shrill, wavering chant that was more of a whimper, as Pardoe sang: "I'll Take You Home Again, Kathleen."

A Small Favor

When Franz realized that he was not alone in the house, his first impulse was to withdraw. Quiet burglary, not violence, was his forte; and to make matters worse, the other party was a woman. An hysterical housewife is never any help to a man in Franz's midnight profession.

As always, he had prepared a sure line of retreat. Although he had entered through a basement window, his first precaution, once inside the building, had been to unfasten, very stealthily, both front and rear doors. Thus, should any emergency arise, Franz could make a bolt for it in either direction.

But the whole situation was confusing. Franz knew that his brain was often muddled; that it didn't work as it had years ago in the little Bavarian town of his childhood. But even so, this woman was not supposed to be on the premises at all. A few days earlier the paper had reported that the family was leaving for Europe. It was quite a shock to find her at home, since Franz had hoped to ransack the place at his leisure.

He was just about to abandon the whole project as a bad job, when he heard the woman sobbing upstairs. It bothered him, that agonized weeping, bringing strong, unpleasant memories to his mind. Motivated by many obscure feelings, Franz crept up the winding stairs, and peeked into the bedroom. He did this by applying an eye very cautiously to the space just below one hinge of the door, which was almost closed.

She was lying on the bed, fully dressed, although it was near midnight. A small, rather round woman, of perhaps thirty-five. Even as he watched, she beat upon the pillow with soft, futile hands and exclaimed, "Oh, God—what can I do now? There's just no way out."

Franz was embarrassed. He usually regarded his wealthy victims as so many nameless moneybags. Robbing them was like bilking a soulless entity—say the transit company. No matter what you took, they had—or easily acquired—more. But here was a rich woman who seemed human and very unhappy.

Even as he pondered this matter, the extension phone rang, and she reached for it in convulsive haste. Franz listened shamelessly, wondering why her dark, tearstained face hurt him inside.

"Yes," she was saying in a low voice. "I'm alone. I let the family go first. I have the money, but how can I possibly explain about my jewels if they—yes, $5,000 in small bills, mostly fifties, just as you said. But please, couldn't you—?"

Whatever plea she had hoped to make remained incomplete, withered by some statement from the other end of the line. Franz recognized the despair in her tones as she said dully: "All right. I'll bring it now. Of course, I'll be alone. Where this time? The old barn on Highway 43, just north of Brinton. Yes, I know the place. I'll leave at once."

Instantly Franz was scuttling downstairs, his rubber soled shoes noiseless on the heavy carpeting. His own car was parked a short distance away, and he meant to tag along. That he was losing a fine chance to loot the house carried no weight with him now. The woman made his muddled brain churn with queer emotions from the past, feelings that were dredged up from levels seldom disturbed these days. Somebody else, also plump, dark, and too often in tears, came to mind. Franz thought of her as he sent his old car racing down the highway behind the woman's sleek import.

Gradually he lessened the distance between them, and noting that she was inclined to dawdle, Franz concluded that it would be better tactics, in any case, to arrive first at the rendezvous, and with luck ahead of the blackmailer, too.

When he reached the old barn, he kept right on for perhaps three hundred yards, pulled off the road, and with unerring steps worked his way back to the meeting place. His old skill as a gamekeeper was still there, for he crept up to the barn without making a leaf rustle. And even in the bright moonlight, it would have taken a keen eye to follow his movements.

A few moments' competent and silent reconnaissance convinced him that he was first on the scene, and Franz settled down behind a well placed bush to await events.

Scarcely had he made himself comfortable, when the blackmailer appeared on foot, having also left his car elsewhere. He made a brief, stumbling inspection of the area that brought a sneer from Franz, snugly concealed. The man's lumbering footsteps would have alerted any real woodsman a hundred yards off.

For a while the man paced impatiently up and down, lighting one cigarette after another, and swearing now and then in an undertone. One of his stubs actually bounced off Franz's cropped head, but he didn't stir. Finally the blackmailer stiffened and stood at gaze as the thrumming of a distant car increased in volume. "About time," he muttered, flattening himself against the barn.

The big car rolled to a stop, and Franz could see the woman get out, her whole attitude one of reluctance. Satisfied that she was alone, the man went to meet her, and Franz, moving like a shadow, followed within easy earshot.

"You didn't hurry any," the blackmailer snapped.

"I'm too nervous to drive fast," she said in a shaky voice. "I didn't dare. I couldn't. Not tonight."

"You brought the money?" It was more of a statement than a question.

"Yes." And then with a pathetically feeble attempt at firmness, "But it must be positively the last payment. My jewelry is gone, and I simply can't raise another penny without getting caught."

"Too bad," he said, blandly malicious. "I'll have to tap your husband from now on." He caught her little gasp, and snickered unpleasantly.

"But you promised—"

"Of course. But you just said you would stop paying, and that releases me from any part of the bargain. Besides, I promised just to keep you from unnecessary worrying. Really, it was a favor." He paused to peer at her cynically in the moonlight. "Pity you're not my type, or something could be arranged. *I'm* not full of prejudice. If you were a few years younger ..."

Franz's heartbeat speeded up. There was a tone in the blackmailer's voice he had heard often before. Sometimes tenor; then again, bass. Even contralto. It was a note of pleasure; the purr of a cat with an injured mouse to play with. Franz fought an irrational urge to run, to cringe, to scream, to beg, to turn to wood and be as invulnerable to pain.

"You see," the man went on, choosing his words with obvious relish, like a ham actor on display, "what I'm selling is my silence. No letter, nothing in writing to change hands. Just a stray bit of knowledge that's my old age insurance. Since it's in my mind, I can't lose it or have it stolen. Pay me regularly, and nobody else in the world who cares needs ever to know. Especially your blue-blooded husband from dear old Vuhginny—"

"Please," she said faintly. "I'll try to make another payment next month."

"Do that little thing," he mocked her. "Or don't. It's all the same to me. Your husband would pay gladly. And now, dear lady, you clear away from here first, so I can see you out of sight before I leave. You might get desperate enough to follow me some time, and I prefer not to take chances. Some of your family might revert to type and slice me up." He thrust the packet of bills into a coat pocket, and withdrew to the shadow of the barn. The woman stood there for a moment, as if paralyzed, then with slow, stumbling steps returned to her car. The blackmailer watched her, and as she drove away, began to walk at an angle towards the highway. He was humming a tune, and his stride was jaunty.

He had covered barely twenty yards when a sharp point pricked the back of his neck, and a strange voice said: "Put your hands behind your back—quick!" Frightened and bewildered, he hastily complied, and Franz methodically tied them with a piece of cord. "Now march! Over to that patch of moonlight. I want to see your face."

Moving awkwardly, the man did so, and Franz studied him gravely. It was a full face, jowly and pale, but quite respectable in appearance.

Not at all the features of a desperate criminal. Not like Muller, for example, or the brutal Hartmann. More like the little clerk, Schick, who tortured the rabbits he poached, and later tortured humans.

"What do you want?" the blackmailer demanded sullenly. "Who the devil are you?"

"I heard your conversation with the gracious lady," Franz replied. He spoke very gently.

"Are you after a cut?"

"Why should I cut? I need only to take."

This was so obviously true that the other didn't reply.

"It seems you have a secret to sell," Franz said. "I like secrets. Tell me yours. A secret worth $5,000 a month is most unusual even in this so-rich country."

"So you know the arrangement." The blackmailer was bitter. "She sent you, that two-timing—! And I thought she wouldn't tell anybody her precious secret. Well, it won't work. If you take back the money, I'll squeeze double out of her next time. Unless—" He broke off as a disturbing thought came to him. Fear was strong in his voice now. "You can't—she wouldn't let you—not Mrs. Cary. Killing me wouldn't do any good. It's all written down. I swear it. And with instructions in case of my death—"

"Stop these foolish lies," Franz interrupted contemptuously. "Tell me the big secret, the $5,000 secret."

"No," was the hoarse reply. "She never sent you. She wouldn't want anybody else to catch on. You're just trying to muscle in. Well, you can't pull that on me."

Franz's voice became cold and venomous. "You will tell me the truth—all of it."

"Like hell. This is *my* racket."

Franz spoke almost in a whisper, as if reminiscing. "Fool! I've seen better men than you eaten alive by dogs while the band played pretty waltz music to drown their shrieks. I have tried to forget those times, but it is hard, and you remind me of *them*." The knife glinted in the moonlight as he moved forward, and the blackmailer seemed to shrink inside his clothes.

"Don't! Lay off. I'll tell you. Man, I don't like knives."

90

"Talk, then, and no lies. I can smell a lie. For years I was with people who lied to live. There is nothing about lying I don't know. The lie with the mouth; the lie with the eye; the lie with the whole body."

The other's face was damp now, despite the cool night air, and his words came in a turgid stream.

"That woman—Mrs. Cary—she's married to a real high class guy from Virginia. He thinks she's an orphan, but her mother was one of the biggest madams in New Jersey. I found it out just by luck; the old lady covered her tracks pretty slick, sending the kid to a fancy Connecticut finishing school and all. She's dead now, and the other relatives would never spill the beans, but Mrs. Cary knows what a good private eye could come up with if somebody pointed him in the right direction. There's a birth certificate, and hospital records, census—plenty to go on. If her husband ever found out, he'd raise merry hell with both of them. His family back in Virginia would have kittens! There's money in it—a mint. I'll cut you in, but let's don't spoil the racket, huh?"

"I don't understand," Franz said humbly. "What is a 'madam,' and why is Mrs. Cary to blame for her mother?"

"Man, you are square!" the blackmailer groaned. He made a hasty explanation, and Franz began to shake in turn. "To Cary and his crowd, a person's ancestry is the works—that bunch goes back to the Revolution. Bad enough his picking an orphan, but when she turns out to have a madam for her ma—bro-ther!"

There was a moment's pregnant silence as Franz's thoughts went back through the years to Berlin.

"I must tell you something now," Franz breathed. "About how they warned my father he was married to a woman of inferior race. He let them take my mother; he was a coward and a pig. My brothers and sisters were too young to know, but I was fourteen, and when I learned what they did to her—" His voice became almost inaudible. "A little, frightened woman, dark and gentle—so very gentle."

"Look, take the damn money and let me get out of here," the blackmailer said. "I'll lay off her if that's the way you want it."

Suddenly he jerked his arms powerfully, and his hands were free of the cord. He lunged forward desperately, and his shoulder struck Franz a numbing blow.

When he returned to the big house, it was six in the morning, and sunny. Franz rang the bell, and when the woman appeared at the door, showing all the signs of a sleepless night, he handed her the package.

"For you," he said. "A man gave it to me and told me to tell you— yes, he told me to tell you that your secret was safe, that he wouldn't ever say another word."

She recognized the wrapping, and her eyes widened incredulously.

"You mean?— B-But, I—" She broke off in horror as she saw his hands, so terribly blistered and torn.

Franz sheepishly put them behind his back.

"Oh," he smiled, "I had to dig—without tools; just a fence stake, and my flesh is much too soft these days."

"Please come in, and let me bandage them. It's the least I can do"

Franz shrugged. "If you like," he said. "It was only a small favor I did you."

She thought he meant delivering the package, but Franz was thinking of a different chore altogether.

Bet with a Witch

I hadn't known Cynthia Wade very long, but nevertheless I liked her. It goes without saying that my admiration was physical as well as emotional but I had sense enough to see there wasn't much chance along that line.

Cynthia was a tall, lithe blonde, with a spectacular figure that attracted every male eye within a radius of five hundred feet. Once I had seen a blind guy, who must have been eighty, lean on his cane and sniff the air hungrily when Cynthia undulated past. Not that she was over-endowed in the voluptuous Hollywood fashion; it was more a matter of just enough in the right places, with a rounded firmness and vitality that spelled sex in letters nine feet tall. And ironically, to carry out the advertising analogy, all that promise was as phony as a three-dollar bill.

If Cynthia's tremendous physical appeal had been flaunted, its power would have been far less effective; but there was a certain coolness about her, a child-like wonder in her greenish eyes, that seemed to make her the storybook princess—a woman infinitely desirable, but made of moonlight and illusion rather than solid female flesh. They just could not visualize her rumpled and panting in somebody's convertible. In fact, I doubt if any of her dates ever got beyond the first halfhearted pass or two before being frozen into an unwonted gentility, ashamed of his baser instincts. I know damned well that was the case with me. Men reacted that way, I suppose, because as any good psychologist will tell us, we are the romantic idiots, not women. And if you're thinking no girl could make you behave that way, it's because you haven't met Cynthia.

She could have been married at practically any moment after her sixteenth birthday; instead, and at the ripe age of twenty-five, she didn't even have a steady boyfriend, but just played the field, although entirely on her own terms. If the lack of anything more permanent or exciting in her emotional life ever bothered her, there was no sign of it to me during our brief association. She had her job as a receptionist in a plush suite of Beverly Hills doctors, where her frosty loveliness must have made the male patients forget both their ailments and their wives, in that order.

I met her, by the way, after taking a job as a dental technician in the next office of the medical building where she worked. I'm neither very handsome nor highly predatory, but can be good company when properly motivated. Cynthia was no fool; she had plenty of wit and intelligence. It was worthwhile dating her occasionally, just to have a lot of poor slobs looking at me in envy.

But I'm neither simple-minded nor romantic enough to build my love life around such a woman. When I wanted interesting conversation and envious looks—the first from Cynthia, and the second, usually, from sulky husbands out with their wives—she was perfect. When I needed something a bit more fundamental, there were plenty of other girls.

Often we double-dated, which is how I had a chance to learn something about Cynthia's technique with men, a very educational experience, and quite amusing if you didn't happen to be hooked yourself. Cynthia's sleight of hand was flawless. By just being what she was, the girl did not give an inch unless she really wanted to. There was never a wrestling match to decide the issue. Aware that every man in the place was envying him, Cynthia's date easily survived the shock of being rejected at Cynthia's door. She made it even more tolerable by her treatment of him in public. There, where others were watching, she seemed warm and devoted. It always worked. After all, to be seen in the company of such a radiantly attractive girl did almost as much for a man's morale as actually possessing her. I ought to know, having played her little game a few times myself, and without regrets.

But, as I've said, there were others on my list. That was not the case with Wally Martin. I mentioned earlier that Cynthia had no one steady. That wasn't quite the whole truth. She did have a hanger-on, stubby, gentle, innocent Wally. He had a pinky-yellow complexion, and such small, vague features that his face suggested a peeled nectarine. His eyes were soft, brown, and melancholy, like those of a constipated sheepdog. A fussily neat little man, about thirty, with plump, helpless looking hands, he was the sort who loved children—the grubbier the better—and would go a mile out of his way to help an old woman more capable than himself.

After a while Cynthia told me more about him. They had gone to high school together. Wally had been smitten at the age of seventeen, and never got over it. He had done her math homework, written her term papers, and walked his feet off so that she could use his jalopy. He was now a successful CPA, with money in the bank; but still lived alone, forsaking all others, and no doubt enjoying his queer martyrdom. Almost every day he sent flowers or candy, his only reward an occasional chance to spend a costly evening with her. She kept him at arm's length with near automatic finesse, and fed his candy to the doctors. Not that it was difficult to restrain poor Wally. To him the storybook princess illusion was the very heart of reality. An infrequent kiss, the sort a sister might give a small brother, brightened his whole week.

The possibility of placing his lips against her throat or any of the other highly suitable areas of her body apparently never occurred to him. Not that he'd have made it; I have seen her deflect the attacks of much more experienced men, and so skillfully that they never quite knew what shifted their sights from the bullseye. Wally didn't know his behavior was abnormal; he'd been raised by a puritanical mother. I sometimes wonder how close Wally came to not being born at all; certainly mama couldn't have cared for connubial bliss.

So he just went on, a sort of eunuch tab-picker-upper, never realizing that the only man who impressed Cynthia at all was Dr. Graham, no doubt because he didn't know she existed. The doctor was wedded to his research on tropical diseases, a shocking waste of good beefcake, from what the women were saying.

I know now that there must have been a deep strain of cruelty in Cynthia. Maybe she hated men as a species; I can't be sure. It's possible she took an occasional lover, and even gave herself with abandon; I'm not fool enough to think that because I and some others didn't excite her, nobody could. But certainly she didn't need Wally's fumbling attentions; there were plenty of others happy to play her game and pay her bills without any illusions—people not easily hurt, or who hadn't earned special consideration. It would have been merciful to cut him loose to sink or swim. Without her around, he might have mastered his fixation and found himself some dull, affectionate *hausfrau* to bear the eight or nine kids he hungered for.

Well, she did drop him at last, but in a way that still makes me a little queasy when I think about it. I was there at the time, at least when the nastiness began, although many of the implications escaped me at the critical moment.

It started when Wally phoned to ask—beg would be a better word—for a date with Cynthia. His particular excuse for the great concession on her part was that he had a birthday to celebrate. I happened to be chatting at her desk, and heard the conversation. She had nothing else lined up at the moment, but refused. When he persisted, she finally agreed, telling the poor jerk that she'd already promised me, so that it would have to be a threesome. I told her, in indignant whispers, that it wasn't right to spoil the guy's date with a third party, but she had her way as usual. When she turned those luminous, naive looking eyes toward you, and purred, it was damn near impossible to say no. Looking back now, I'm sure she had the whole business with Wally planned, and wanted me as a witness: somebody to appreciate her fine sadistic coup.

Wally took us to Bragin's, one of the nicer places in town. Nobody gets out of there with anything much left from a fifty-dollar bill. The foolish little man was so infatuated with Cynthia that not even my presence discouraged him. Through several courses of expensive food he pleaded with her to marry him. Pleasantly, her sea-green eyes aglow with some obscure excitement, she rejected him unconditionally. At the same time, she patted his hand, leaned forward to display the satin perfection of her cleavage, and smiled at him in an inviting, cryptic way, luring even as she withheld.

Wally was almost panting; it seemed to him that the moment had finally come; that she must be about to yield in spite of her unequivocal words. He pressed harder, convinced that the possession of this elusive creature was the only thing in the whole world that mattered. The idiot was caught in a self-made mirage. I wanted to snap him out of it with something vulgar, but I hated to butt in. I didn't want lose Cynthia's friendship, and—I'd better admit it—I, too, was partly in the mirage of her glamor.

Then she sprung her trap.

"Wally, dear," she purred in that creamy voice that suggested silver bells. "You've been after me how many years now?"

"Since I was sixteen," he sighed. "I could name the exact day. Twelve long years. And so help me," he added, pink face glowing, "I've never even looked at another girl in all that time."

"I believe you," she said gently, a sly glint in her eyes. I knew that she thought Wally to be a virgin; on one occasion she had described the betraying symptoms to me with almost clinical precision. Very possibly she was right, and poor Wally was one of those rare males who "save themselves" for *the* girl.

"In medieval times," she went on, lips parted, her expression dreamy, "a knight had to undergo some ordeal to win his lady." Her voice had obvious satirical undertones now, but the little fool lapped it up as something quite natural from a princess.

"I'd do anything—you know I would. Just give me the chance."

"But Wally, this is 1963!"

"That doesn't matter."

"I believe you really mean it," she said, suddenly grave, looking at him with new respect. It was beautifully put on, of course, but he was in no state to suspect that. All he knew was that Cynthia seemed to be taking him seriously for once.

"I do mean it. Just try me."

"It wouldn't be fair," she said, in a sober voice. "Too one-sided. Why should *I* risk nothing?"

"What do you mean?" he demanded, puzzled.

"Let's make it a bet, instead. If you win, I'll marry you at once. If I win, there will be a penalty—and no marriage."

"Would you really?" he said. "You mean it?"

"Don't be hasty. The penalty is very severe."

"That doesn't matter. What's the bet?"

She reflected a moment, as if trying to think of something offhand. The lovely, frigid devil; it was all planned in advance, I'm certain.

"I've a wonderful idea," she said brightly, all girlish enthusiasm. "A sort of puzzle. But we'll have to go to my apartment—no, maybe we'd better go to yours, Wally. Then you'll know nothing is rigged up in advance to trick you. Tell me, do you have a broom at home?"

"A broom?" He gaped at her.

"That's right. Just an ordinary broom—any kind."

"There's one around some place. I seldom use it since I bought a vacuum cleaner."

"There speaks the efficient accountant," Cynthia said dryly. "Shall we go?"

Still a little baffled, but elated, too, at the possibilities of this enchanted evening, Wally thrust a handful of bills on the table to pay for the tab. Cynthia hustled us out, although Wally didn't need any urging.

As we drove to his apartment, she began to work on him again. He was blissfully unaware of the dissection, taking it for fair play and solicitude.

"You want to consider this bet very carefully," she said. "I think you're overrating my attractions as a wife."

"Like hell," he retorted gallantly, grabbing for her hand. "I've waited twelve years for you to come around, and it would be worth it ten times over," he added.

"Even so, you may change your mind when you know the risk of losing. I hope your word is good."

"Of course," he said indignantly. "If I lose, I'll pay. Would I welsh on you, of all people?"

"No, I don't think you would," Cynthia said, looking suddenly like a small cat, all wide-eyed softness. She pressed her shoulder against him, and he sat more erect behind the wheel.

Wally's apartment was immaculate. The modern furniture was excellent; the Bracque painting very suitable. Wally began to fuss around preparing drinks, but Cynthia had other fish to fry.

"Please sit down," she told him. "You make me nervous."

Meekly, Wally obeyed. After all, it was delightful to take orders from a princess when she honors your home. Maybe his own princess soon. It was so nauseating I almost lost all my sympathy for the poor little creep.

"Now listen carefully," Cynthia said. "The bet is a puzzle about a broom. If you solve it, I'll marry you any time you say. If you don't, the price will be a stiff one. I've no right to expect you to agree; any man might be afraid." The way she said it, most men would rather have died on the spot than admit to any such fear.

Wally paled a little, as much from excitement, perhaps, to do him justice, as from apprehension.

"I'm not worried," he said stoutly. "A broom, huh? I always thought you were half witch! No mere woman could be so lovely and strange." It was almost prophetic, that remark, but Cynthia ignored it.

"Remember, you don't have to accept the terms at all. I'm not worth it. But you mustn't blame me afterwards—that is, if you lose."

"I'll take my chances," he said. "And don't worry about being blamed. I'm glad of the chance. Now, what's this mysterious bet?"

"First you'd better know the penalty for losing. I want to be absolutely above board." She solemnly fixed her green eyes on him. "A doctor in my office thinks he's finally isolated the virus that causes African encephalitis." She paused, and Wally went livid. "It's impossible to test it on animals. He needs a volunteer. If he doesn't get one, I'm afraid he'll use himself. That would be terrible, because if anything happened to him—" she hesitated for not more than a heartbeat, then went on smoothly "—the research would stop." Her quick recovery didn't fool me. It was Graham she feared for, not the unhappy African natives who might be helped by his work.

"Isn't that Sleeping Sickness?" Wally demanded finally.

"Not necessarily," she reassured him. "Many cases never get to that stage at all. They pull out of it after minor symptoms. I told you, though," she added gravely, "that the penalty was too high; that I wasn't worth the risk."

"That's not so," he said hoarsely. "Besides, I could win, couldn't I?" The naked pleading in his voice was almost unbearable.

"Of course, you could. The bet wouldn't be fair otherwise. Your chance is just as good as mine."

He hesitated for a moment, drawing delay from some hidden reservoir of sanity. It must have occurred to him that no woman was worth such a price, least of all this chilly sadist. But then, I suppose, he couldn't see her as a woman at all. She was a princess right from Ruritania or Zenda.

"Don't be a damn fool, Wally!" I blurted out. "Find another girl. There are thousands of them around who want husbands, not guinea pigs."

Cynthia gave me a sudden glance that flickered like summer lightning. Then she favored Wally with her patrician smile.

"He's perfectly right. Don't bet. The loss is too high compared to the gain. We can still be friends—just as before."

His hungry eyes were fixed on her with a terrible intensity. She was at her best in a skintight sheath that would have made a telephone pole look sexy.

"The virus may not even work," he said hopefully.

"That's very probable," she agreed. "They've never found one before that did. And if it does take, there still isn't much danger, since you'd be treated at once by an expert."

"I'm ready," Wally said, his forehead gleaming with moisture. "What's the puzzle? Or is it some kind of a stunt I have to try?"

"Does he have to agree to solve it without even knowing how tough the thing is?" I protested. "That's not fair. It might be the kind of question that would stump a Harvard professor."

"Not at all. I'll explain first, and he can still back out. I intend to be absolutely honest in this whole thing. Where's that broom, Wally?"

He went to the tiny kitchen, and got it. Cynthia lifted the broom, and seemed satisfied. It was an ordinary one, about five feet long, with neat plastic bristles.

"Hold your hands straight out in front of you," she ordered Wally. Dumbly he obeyed. "Get them level, that's right—parallel to the floor. Now stick out the two forefingers, and fold the others out of the way. I'm going to balance the broom on them."

When she was done, he stood there with the broom horizontal across the two extended fingers. His left forefinger was about five inches from the cluster of bristles, and the right one a foot or so away from it.

"It's very simple, really," Cynthia said. "The question is this: If you hold your arms level, as they are, and move the two extended fingers slowly and smoothly together, to which side will the broom topple?"

"Which side—?" Wally repeated weakly. Then his brow cleared. "I see what you mean. But surely—"

"Before you say anything, or try it, is our bet on?"

He reflected for a moment. I could almost read his mind, because no doubt we were both asking ourselves the same questions. It seemed obvious—too obvious—that the moment those forefingers began to approach each other, the heavy, sweeping end of the broom was bound to drop. But when is a puzzle that simple? Wally, like me, wanted to believe his eyes, to trust common sense, but his knowledge of past parlor tricks urged him to shun the obvious. Maybe, no matter how unreasonable it seemed, the lighter side was the one. He stood there, pale, his plump face moist, agonizing over the problem.

"Then what's your answer?"

Cynthia herself was more animated than I'd ever seen her before. The wide green eyes were feline in their luminescence; her whole sleek body seemed made of compressed steel springs, and her red mouth was open just enough to display the small, glittering teeth. She looked dangerous and yet highly attractive, a lovely pagan sexually stimulated at the Roman Games.

"The heavy side will drop," Wally said with surprising firmness.

"Do you mean the bristly part?"

"Yes."

"Try it now," Cynthia commanded. "Easy—easy; fingers level." Her voice told us nothing. For all I knew then, he'd guessed correctly, after all.

101

Wally began to move his two fingers together; that is, he tried. Then his watery eyes blinked foolishly as he became aware of the joker. Only the right forefinger progressed to the left. It steadily approached the left one, which did not move at all. It wasn't until the right finger was within a few inches of the left, that both moved together. They met at the exact balance point of the broom.

There was a moment of pregnant silence; then Wally let the broom slide from his fingers. It fell to the floor with a crash, and he said heavily: "Guess I lose."

"I'm sorry," Cynthia said, but I could sense the elation behind her mask of compassion.

He was looking at her with clouded eyes.

"What do I do?"

"Be at Dr. Graham's office tomorrow morning at ten. Tell him I sent you, but better not go into detail. He's anxious for a volunteer to ask many questions, but if he knew you were paying off a bet, he might refuse to go ahead with the tests. There'll be a release to sign, I imagine."

"Well," Wally said in a futile effort to be casual, "at least I don't have any dependents to worry about. No heirs at all, in fact."

She walked over to him, put her hands on his shoulders, and kissed his mouth. Wally accepted what seemed to him an accolade, or at least a consolation prize.

"I'll be there in the morning," Wally said. "And now, let's call it an evening, shall we?"

I saw Cynthia only once more after that, since I quit my job expressly to avoid her. But we met briefly in the foyer of a movie theatre. It was there she told me, quite calmly, that Wally had encephalitis. Unfortunately, he was highly susceptible, so that the coma stage came quickly. Maybe they would pull him out of it in time, but right now he was conscious only at intervals, and due for a long siege in the hospital. It was a great victory for medical science, no doubt, and a bigger one for Cynthia, I inferred, since she made it clear that Dr. Graham saw her much better now than anything he'd ever spotted under the microscope. I'm not sure, after what happened, that he's any more ethical than she, so my hunch that he'd have been better off staring at microbes doesn't make me bleed for the guy. It's comforting to think that she may have plans for him, in the long run, no more pleasant than those she had for poor Wally.

Although it wasn't my business, there was one question I had to ask.

"What if Wally had guessed the right answer?"

She smiled. "Very unlikely. Nobody but a sharp physicist could do that offhand. The engineer who showed me the trick said that out of several hundred bright science students at the university, only a handful predicted the result."

I knew very well how right she was. A mathematician I know analyzed the thing for me. It seems that when you begin, the heavier part of the broom presses harder on the left finger, so that only the right is free to move. As it approaches the right one, the left gradually meets more resistance; and when the pressure on each finger is the same, then both are free to move together, inevitably meeting at the balance point. Seems simple, when explained; but not when confronted by the trick for the first time.

"But what if he had been lucky somehow?"

"Then I'd have married him, of course. It would never have been consummated. Oh, not that I'd welsh; I have a few scruples. But I know Wally's type. He's in love with an illusion. He's had me on a pedestal so long he'd have been quite impotent in bed. He thinks he wants me very badly, and would try to take me, but he'd never have made it—not in a million years. And especially without my help. He wouldn't get that; Wally's hands would make my skin crawl. After the first night or two, he'd have been happy to give me a divorce and hide his face somewhere. As it is, in spite of that unfortunate bet, Wally still clings to his illusion. You see, I happen to know he's made me his heir."

Yes, I liked Cynthia at first. I don't any more, although she's as nice to look at as ever. But she's a witch, with the power to fascinate and destroy. Don't tell me there are no such things. I know better, even if Wally doesn't.

A Change for the Better

There is something peculiarly frustrating about a blackmailer, as compared with other criminals. Unlike a thief, a swindler, or a sex-fiend, he is just as dangerous behind bars as when free. He sells something a dozen times, but still retains a clear title to it. If the victim buys a negative, he may be sure copies have been made, so that the transaction settles exactly nothing. And when information is peddled, the situation is even less satisfactory, since such a commodity can pass to a hundred people without leaving the blackmailer's possession at all. It is still his to sell again—for life.

For life—only in that phrase lies the criminal's vulnerability. Dead men tell no tales. Not in person, but no blackmailer worth his salt ever puts his own life on the line. Always there is a letter, left in a safety deposit box, or with a friend, and marked: To be opened in case of my death. It is made quite plain to the victim that by killing his tormentor, he gains nothing whatever. At worst, exposure; at best, a new leech to deal with.

Gene Sinclair was a blackmailer, and one of the best. He paid well, himself, for secrets, and then put on the squeeze. He bought from people too timid or inexperienced to use the knowledge themselves: maids, cooks, hairdressers, and the like. He picked his victims with great care. They had to have money above all. A wealthy man or woman with a place in society to protect—that was always good. Better still, if they had children to shield from some terrible truth. Occasionally, but not often, you could even find a child willing to be blackmailed in order to protect his parents, especially if they were old and sick, and still thought of a forty-year-old man as their baby.

Sinclair was not just an ordinary blackmailer, that is to say, a grubby, small-souled person capable only of this most cowardly crime. He was intelligent, witty, personable, well read, and even lovable to those who didn't probe very deeply. In fact, he had no soul at all, and nerves of brass. He lived well, tipped generously, and subsidized young blondes who liked convertibles, furs, and gambling at Las Vegas. It was nothing but the best for Gene Sinclair. And, contrary to all the homilies ever written, he slept ten dreamless hours each night.

At this moment he was making a collection at one of his best sources. The young woman who sat facing him in the living room of the big house had a pinched look about her nostrils. He had always admired her eyes, which were large and the blue of woodsmoke. The rest of her wasn't bad, either, Sinclair reflected, not for the first time. A slim figure, but rounded in the best places; long legs that didn't sprawl, as they often seemed to on the Las Vegas blondes; and a look of well scrubbed elegance that came from generations of money.

"You told me last time I'd not be bothered again for a month," she said bitterly.

"And I meant it," he assured her, showing white teeth in a killing smile. "But roulette just isn't my game, and yet I always succumb."

"So I must finance your gambling."

"I'm afraid so. Right now you're my only client with sufficient cash."

"You're quite wrong. I have no money left. Maybe next month—"

"Let's not waste time. Your father is the best neurosurgeon in the country. Why, that operation on Prince Fuad must have netted him at least five thousand dollars, and probably more."

"I can't ask him for any more. I just can't."

"Would you rather I went to your fiancé? I'm sure he'd like to know that his bride-to-be had an illegitimate child at the age of fifteen. His parents would be even more interested; I understand they think of the Cabots and Lodges as upstarts."

The blue eyes flashed.

"If George knew about you, he'd beat you to death."

"Oh, he could do it, easily enough. A top athlete," Sinclair said thoughtfully. "Not that I'm a weakling; but he's in fine condition, no doubt, while I've been dissipating. Blondes and gambling are not exactly muscle builders. But dear George would never be so foolish, would he? You know my ground rules. Give me any trouble, and my charges go up in proportion."

"He'd kill you!"

"That would be twice as silly. I've left a letter with a friend, telling him just where to find my secret files. It's to be opened in case of my death, a very obvious precaution."

Her shoulders slumped in defeat. It was inevitable, yet always gave him pleasure. The worm twisted and writhed, but invariably found itself under the boot heel.

"Unless you get me some cash in a hurry, Lisa, honey, I'll have to charge for overtime."

"All right; you win. I've no idea how I'll explain it to my father …" Her voice trailed off in a sob.

"That won't be necessary."

She turned with a cry, and Sinclair stiffened.

"Dad! I thought you were at the hospital."

The tall man, slightly stooped, gave her a reassuring smile, but his eyes, a much colder blue than hers, remained fixed on the blackmailer.

"I've always known about my daughter's mistake," he said evenly. "She was only a child at the time. Possibly George's parents would understand, too, but I can't risk it."

She stared at him in amazement.

"But all these years—you never said—"

"Why should I? I knew your visit to Marilyn was not just a vacation; remember, I'm a doctor. It seemed best to let you think the secret was your own. Why do you suppose the adoption went through so smoothly and without publicity?"

"Still," Sinclair drawled, "you let her pay me. Very sensible. Now why not save the heart-to-heart talk until I've left. Just pay up, and I'll intrude no longer."

"I think not," the doctor said, his eyes glacial in their stare. "I didn't put in this rather melodramatic appearance just to act as paymaster. You are finished, Sinclair."

The blackmailer's lips narrowed, and he gave a grimace of distaste that was almost comical in its emphasis.

"Do I have to spell it out again? How can people be so stupid? I don't just carry information here"—he tapped his head—"but always leave a letter with somebody. So if you're thinking of killing me, just forget it. The moment my death is known, no matter what the cause, my friend will open that letter. And then he'll either spill the beans, or take over where I left off."

"I've no intention of killing you," the surgeon said calmly. "As you've pointed out, that's no solution."

His daughter was watching him in bewilderment.

"But, Dad. I don't see how—"

"Leave it to me, Lisa."

He pulled a gun from his pocket. The muzzle pointed squarely at Sinclair. The blackmailer shook his head in disbelief.

"I really ought to print a little booklet," he said irritably. "Didn't I just explain the situation? You can't kill me, and I don't want to hurt you; I never carry a gun. So just put that thing away; it makes me nervous."

"I wouldn't take your word for anything," the doctor said. "Go over to the wall, and assume the position. I'm sure you know what it is; they use it on all the TV programs. Move!" he added sharply, waving the gun. "Hands against the wall, feet away from it; you know what I mean."

Sinclair looked at the grim face again; the eyes seemed filmed with ice. It was almost certain the old boy didn't mean to shoot, but if pushed, who could tell? The blackmailer knew character, and this surgeon could be dangerous. Maybe he had some idea of killing him and hiding the body. Conrad wouldn't open the letter if Sinclair merely vanished. But the doctor wouldn't know that; besides, not even he could dispose of a body that easily. Assuming an expression of bored tolerance, the blackmailer went to the wall.

Cautiously, the old man searched him, finding no weapon.

"Just stay put," he ordered, and went to a large secretaire. He unlocked a door, and as Lisa watched wide-eyed, took out two pairs of handcuffs. Deftly, with his surgeon's fingers, he cuffed Sinclair's hands behind him. "Feet together now," he directed, and when the command was obeyed, used the other pair of cuffs on the man's ankles.

"This is all very silly," Sinclair said angrily, conscious now that no matter what happened, Dollie would have left the Eagle Bar in a huff. Pity; she was a tasty dish. "It's just going to cost you extra."

"There are other ways of shutting a man up besides killing him," the surgeon said.

"What d'you mean? Gonna cut my tongue out? I can write, you know!"

"I assumed as much. And even if completely paralyzed, you could work out a code with your eyelids, or something. You see, I've given quite a bit of thought to you."

Sinclair felt his neck hairs tingle, and his back was suddenly cold.

"You mean you thought of deliberately paralyzing me! That would be inhuman!"

Even as he said it, and before the doctor's ironic chuckle, he realized the fatuity of the remark.

"A ruthless animal like you," the surgeon said, "never understands that some day, some place, he'll meet an even more ruthless animal—and one with greater ingenuity. As for being inhuman, let me tell you something, Sinclair. This morning I had to blind a four-year-old girl. She had a glioma, a brain tumor, and if it stayed in, she would die. It was her optic nerve or her life. Do you know what that poor child said she came out of the anesthetic? She cried: "Mommy! Mommy! I can't wake up!" She doesn't even know what blindness is. Now what do you think your life means in comparison with hers? Damn little, believe me; damn little."

"What are you talking about? Blinding me won't solve anything, you old fool!"

"You missed the point. Who said anything about blinding you? I was commenting on the relative value of life; no matter what people say, it's not an absolute. No, I'm not going to hurt your sight. A blackmailer lives by his memory."

"Dad!" Lisa exclaimed, her face chalk white. "You can't!"

108

"Oh, but I can; I must; and I will. Why, it might even make a decent fellow out of him!"

Thoroughly alarmed, Sinclair attempted to get to the door, but the hobbles made him take a crashing fall. He lay there half-stunned, and the old doctor, moving like a panther, closed in, hypo in hand. Before the blackmailer could resist, the needle jabbed relentlessly home into his arm.

"Just relax now," he said in an ironic tone. "You won't feel a thing. But when you come to, your memory will be gone."

"No, don't!" Sinclair begged. "I'll go away! I'll never bother you again!"

"Of course, your word is good enough for me," was the quietly savage reply.

"They'll find out what you did! You'll go to prison."

"Not likely. Assuming a thorough investigation, a good man might spot the brain damage, but it'll never be traced to me. I'll keep you in my private surgery here until the very small wound is healed. It takes only a long needle through a corner of the eye-socket to do the business, you know. And if I slip a little, you may have some other minor disabilities—say a dragging leg, a few tics, a touch of muscular dystrophy, but it won't be malicious—just an unfortunate accident."

"The letter!" Sinclair gasped, fighting to remain conscious.

"Ah, yes, the letter giving the location of your secret files. I wonder where they might be? A small office in some quiet business neighborhood; or maybe you prefer a big and busy building, where nobody can meddle. No matter; you'll tell me where they are."

"Look, let's make a deal. I'll take you to the files. You can destroy the birth certificate, all the papers."

"Sorry," the doctor said. "Not when your real files are in your head."

"Sooner or later my friend will open that letter. You can't win against me."

"You're wrong. I'm going to put enough scopolamine into you to make the sphinx talk. You picked the wrong man to keep secrets from, Sinclair. Truth serum and a spot of hypnosis will do the job nicely. Sweet dreams! He's gone under, Lisa."

"Dad," the girl said shakily. "Are you really going to operate?"

"You can't beat a blackmailer by using kid gloves. Remember Mike Garrity, the one they say is the cleverest thief alive?"

"Yes. He had that simply beautiful child. Janie, wasn't it?"

"Right. When I saved her life, I made a friend. After Sinclair talks—and he will—I can depend on Garrity to get to those files and clean 'em out. And he'd die before telling anybody about it."

A chilly smile touched his lips.

"In a way, we're helping Sinclair, too; giving him needed therapy. After all, was anybody more in need of a massive personality change?"

The Emperor's Dogs

At the funeral of Ottavio Visconti, George Nolan joined the sheriff, and by asking a few questions, idly and at random, was drawn into a case more horrible by far than any ever officially assigned to him as an insurance investigator.

Ironically enough, he wasn't even there in his professional capacity, but merely as a man who had long wanted to own a small ranch. A friend had tipped him off that Visconti's place, a very desirable property, was to be sold at auction, since the heirs were city folks who wouldn't live there. Nolan hoped to find a rare bargain.

He had never met Visconti, and attended the funeral only because most of the town was there, including the sheriff, who, according to the friend, was a good source of information about the ranch, since he sold real estate on the side. There was quite a crowd in the little cemetery; evidently Visconti had been well liked.

"He was a fine man," Sheriff Logan said, when the ceremony was over, and the mourners began to disperse. "Pretty young to die, too; but he just kinda faded away after losing his wife and kid so close together. Had no more interest in living, I'd say. Didn't seem to care about the ranch; even stopped reading all them fancy-back books he had. Liked Roman history, Otto did. Was one writer—fellow named Gibbon—he talked about a lot. Old Miz Dingle—she painted some, and made stuff from clay—she said he looked just like one of them Roman emperors himself. Forget the name: Hadrium, or something. She made a head supposed to be his—Otto's, I mean. Can't say it was much like him, myself. But I ain't an artist. Nor no reader, I guess. Anyhow, Otto just moped around afterwards. He kinda lost his interest in all those things."

It was at this point that Nolan got himself involved.

"How'd it happen?" he asked. "Losing his family."

"Well," Logan said, "his wife died of cancer. That's natural, in a way, and a man can live with it. But the little girl, Gina—that's another story." He spat. "Luther Hoag, he done it, the worthless skunk. Drove his truck right smack through a bunch of kids waiting for the school bus. Killed three, including Gina, and crippled five others. It was just about the worst sight I've seen in forty years as sheriff, and we've had bad accidents on the highway, believe me.

"No excuse for this one, except that Hoag was mean when sober and crazy-wild when drunk, like he was then. Got off with manslaughter, too; that's the hell of it. Managed to have his trial away from town, where they didn't know him. Had a good lawyer and lots of luck, too. Served about eighteen months—no, less'n that; maybe fifteen. Claimed the brakes went bad. Then he come back here, bold as brass. Nobody would talk to him, but a fat lot he cared; had no friends to start with. Mean, tight, and a big bully. Weighed two-fifty, not all fat; a real bull." He spat again. "Good riddance. He sure got what was coming to him, Hoag did. Act of God, I call it. Couldn't be nothing else."

"What happened to him?"

"Craziest thing. Act of God, like I said. Had to be. There was a pack of wild dogs around, killing deer and stock, too. Dunno where they come from. People leave a dog behind when they move, sometimes. Then a few dogs never do like being tame; they just look for a chance to bust loose, same as bad men.

"Anyhow, one afternoon when Hoag was walking down Highway 43, like always—the old dirt road to his place—this pack musta jumped him. They tore him to pieces; it was a horrible thing—almost as bad as those kids after his truck plowed into 'em. Gotta give Luther credit, though; he was tough to the end. Strangled two of 'em, he did; barehanded. A Shepherd and a Doberman; big dogs, vicious, from the looks of 'em. But the others—musta been five or six more in the pack—they were too much even for a bull like Hoag. Chopped him to shreds; I ain't kidding a bit. Funny, too; they ate a lot of him. Dogs don't usually do that—not even a wild bunch on the loose. Kill, yes;

that's their fun. These musta been crazy and starved. Guess the deer was too hard to run down. Tame dogs don't seem to get the trick of it, no matter how hard they try. Wolves can do it fine.

"It was funny, too. We caught most of 'em later, and they didn't seem so wild then. Some came up wagging, to be shot; that's a fact. That's why I say the good Lord musta set 'em all on Hoag. They never bothered nobody else—no people, I mean; just cattle."

Nolan had the strong constructive imagination vital to success in his profession. He could visualize the unpleasant incident all too clearly, and shrank from the scenes presented to his third, inner eye: the deserted road, the big, arrogant, unpopular Hoag heading down it towards his lonely house—and then the unexpected assault by a pack of savage beasts. Nolan hastily turned his thoughts elsewhere.

As for the sheriff's theology, which obviously stemmed from the Old Testament, that was not for him at all. A vengeful God had no place in Nolan's universe. There were only stupid, callous people, who let tame dogs run wild, and failed to corral them until it was too late.

But the matter didn't touch him personally; it was merely a sordid irrelevance unrelated to his search for a bargain ranch.

The next morning, with the sheriff's blessing and the necessary keys, he drove out for a look at the property. "Nobody there now," Logan told him. "A couple of relatives will be down later for the auction. Me, I'd keep the place and live on it, but they like the city and crowds; takes all kinds."

Nolan found the ranch easily enough, and was mildly distressed at the shape it was in. Clearly, having once been almost a model spread, if small, it had been completely neglected of late—since Visconti's loss, no doubt.

Because it was nearest, he began with the big barn, approving its tight construction and roominess. It was messy inside, with all sorts of junk scattered around. Big clean up needed here, he thought.

Not one man in thousands would have noticed the things that drew his immediate attention; and only a trained investigator with a probing mind could have made the inferences suggested by them. But Nolan was used to looking for evidence, whether of arson, murder, or suicide. He could spot the surviving fragments of a device used to start a fire;

or the vague signs that hinted at homicide, and often with only a few sharp glances. Part of it was talent; but most of the knack came from the arduous training of all his faculties.

Now, in the gloomy barn, he saw a big pile of broken lumber and heavy hardware cloth. And there was the ghost of an odor—old and faint, but specific. It was the latter that struck home, because no other stimulus jogs the human memory so quickly and effectively as a remembered scent. Burning leaves; baking bread; a girl's perfume— nothing in print or speech will have such an impact on the consciousness.

Nolan examined the wood and screening, inventing a theory they might fit. He came up very quickly with the only plausible answer. Once these items had belonged to a set of cages; of that there could be no doubt. Added to the faint odor of dog, they began to make a case— one that he didn't really want to pursue, but was unable to resist. It simply wasn't in his nature to leave such a puzzle half-solved.

At that moment, as he stared blank-eyed at the pile of debris, a sudden memory came back to him. Mr. Seyler, the Latin teacher in high school, and how one day, with wet-lipped relish, he had read them an item from Gibbon—an account of some mad Roman emperor who loved to see criminals torn apart by starved hounds. And Visconti knew his Gibbon, Nolan thought, quelling a brief shudder.

But the evidence was still only fragmentary. Cages were not enough; they failed to explain so many things. Then he saw, through a dusty window, the big panel truck behind the barn, and went around for a look.

A careful examination of the vehicle's bed and sides told an interesting story. There were screw-holes and other marks that made Nolan nod slowly as comprehension came. Most significant were the grooves above the tailgate; they suggested a sliding door. Finally, there was still a pulley fixed over the cab of the truck.

Thoughtfully, he went back into the barn, peering about half aimlessly. Then he stooped to pick up a long, narrow stick. Fastened to one end was a piece of stiff wire, two inches long, and filed to a needle point. He studied it, face dark, and felt his neck hairs prickle as understanding came. It's not always an advantage to have strong powers of visualization. Slowly, but systematically, as if etched upon the fabric of his brain by acid, one drop at a time, a grim series of pictures appeared.

He entered Visconti's mind, knowing his situation and probable mood. The bereaved man sees Hoag returning after a few months in prison, unchanged, presumably unrepentant. Wife gone, child gone, Visconti has nothing left that matters but his hate and a dream of revenge.

Hoag is clearly a criminal—a monster who murders children and then has no pain at his heart. In the days of the Roman Empire, they had suitable punishments for such men. Today, one pleads bad brakes and wins more sympathy than the victim.

But here in town, they all knew the car wasn't to blame. Those on the scene had noted Hoag's flushed, blotchy face; his uncoordinated movements; his foolish grinning even in the midst of death. Obviously, he had been drunk, and not for the first time. Because of that, little Gina, sunny and beautiful, is dead. And the others, too—her friends and playmates. There is a price to be paid for such a deed.

Nolan looked at the evidence again. Visconti had built some cages—about seven, he guessed. They were heavy and strong, but not oversize. Just right to hold a large dog securely without permitting it to thrash against the sides. Then, too, the less room, the worse the animal's temper in the end.

Where would he get such dogs? That was easy to answer. Visconti would merely drive to some distant communities, and visit their shelters. He might even say that as a rancher, he preferred a big, vicious brute for a good watchdog. But, in any case, he'd pick the largest animals available—the Boxers, Dobermans and German Shepherds. And only one at a time. Nobody must suspect that he was building up a pack. He would find a suitable dog, bring it home to the barn; and then, the next day, in a different place, where he was unknown, get another.

After that, Nolan reflected, the method was obvious. The animals were penned up individually, so they couldn't fight each other, and then deprived of all food. Here, he looked down at the stick again. In his mind's eye, the investigator could see Visconti, blind of all suffering but his own, repeatedly stabbing his captives with the goad, working them up to a gnashing, frothing rage against him and the whole world of humans.

Finally, there was the mechanical problem of improvising a quick release to be operated from a safe position in the cab of the truck. He must have used a sliding panel; a tug on the rope would raise it, opening all the cages at once.

Visconti knew, of course, the habits of his prospective victim. And so, on that sunny afternoon, as Hoag came down the road, the truck passed him—or was waiting there. He would recognize it, and might even plan to mumble a few words to Visconti; perhaps the big, inarticulate man wanted to say he was sorry. Nobody would ever know. When he was a few yards away, and puzzled by the barks and snarls, Visconti pulled on the release cord. Seven huge dogs, starved and raging, leaped from their cages. Nolan, as if he had been there, felt a spurt of acid burn his throat, sent up by a churning stomach.

He left the barn and went to the house, although he had an uneasy feeling this place would never suit him now. It was poisoned, haunted. No, he would not make a bid for this ranch, bargain though it might be.

The house itself was close, dusty and much too quiet—a dead thing. He went through it on tiptoe, his heart full of pity. There was a photograph of the three Viscontis on the huge Bechstein piano. The woman was plump and dark, full-lipped and sweet of face. Gina was a little lighter in complexion—an elfin child, thin and big-eyed. And Visconti himself, Nolan saw, with a thrill of horror, did resemble a Roman emperor, with his strong, massive features, including a craggy nose, and more than a hint of arrogance. Surely, the investigator thought, the name was ancient; perhaps the blood of some mad Roman tyrant still flowed through Visconti veins.

There was conscious intellectual power in the man's face, too; and further evidence of it all about the house. In addition to his library, mostly well-bound classics in English, Italian and French, there was a collection of chamber music for the hi-fi, a medical microscope and a fine darkroom. Obviously, Ottavio Visconti had not been a simple rancher, but a man of many interests and high culture.

Among the books, few were more worn from loving use than the six-volume set of Gibbon's *The Decline and Fall of the Roman Empire*. Nolan picked up one of these, riffled the pages idly, put it back, and tried another. A photograph slid out, fluttering to the floor. When he stooped for it, and caught a first glimpse of the subject, the shock froze him, awkwardly bent over.

The picture, in full color, a sharp and glossy Ektachrome enlargement, had been taken from the cab of the truck, through the windshield. He recognized the radiator cap, fuzzily out of focus, because it was too close to the camera.

Very clear, however, was the scene on the road. Only a man with a hate-frozen heart could have steadied a delicate instrument and aimed it so precisely in such circumstances.

There was the giant Hoag, sprawling on the ground, his face a mask of terror and despair, with one gaunt German Shepherd dead beside him, a frothing Doberman gripped by the throat in his thick hands, and the other five brutes tearing at him with bloody jaws.

Nolan burned the picture in the fireplace; he didn't stay to hunt for the negative. To hell with it; let the relatives take over. All he wanted now was to get back to the city.

Mr. Kang vs. the Demon

A first cause is never easy to find. In the case of Mr. Kang versus the Demon, however, it is possible to come close. The blame belongs mostly to the cartoonists who brighten the dull pages of certain national magazines. For years they have been drawing the typical Man from Mars as a plump, big-headed, quasi-human individual with spindly legs and an expression of bland disbelief of what he saw here on Earth. To be sure, he was apt to have small antennae on his bald dome, and other minor divergencies from the anatomy of Homo sapiens, but often enough he resembled your Uncle Wilbur at the age of sixty—that unmarried, prissy one, who looked just like a neutered cat, so well preserved, sleek, and sterile.

Yes, it was the fault of those cartoonists, and Mr. Kang's own build, of course, that must have put the Demon on his track. Mr. Kang had a flabby torso shaped like a large fig, pointed end up. On the skinny neck, apparently straining it to the point of causing a permanent oscillation, was a huge head, largely pink scalp. His features were so small and bland that a more literate boy would have thought of Humpty Dumpty; but the Demon never read anything except comic books of the most lurid type. Finally, Mr. Kang had a wide, froglike mouth which nobody had ever seen opened in a smile, or indeed at all, since the little man habitually hissed and sputtered his words from between clenched lips.

In some neighborhoods even an eccentric individual may dwell in peace, although frozen out socially. But Mr. Kang had moved to an area of transients and unskilled laborers, many of them the rejected, the futile, the incompetent, and the bitter elements of the community as a whole. They worked irregularly, drank large quantities of cheap liquor, and raised numerous imps which they thought were children. One of these, the Demon, soon became Mr. Kang's scourge.

The boy's real name was Henry Gordon Bates, but at the age of nine, while attempting to capture and torment a cat, he had been ignominiously routed by a dirty old lady who screamed while brandishing a mop: "Get away from Fluffy, you little Demon, or I'll break every bone in your body!" At least, that was the core of her threat; she had embellished it with fifty adjectives learned in as many dives, most of them having once employed her as a B Girl. None of the words she used was unfamiliar to the child she drove off.

After that, the Demon acquired a small following, and became the official nuisance of the neighborhood. His ingenuity in devising frightfulness was unsurpassed; in addition, he had courage and a forbidding scowl too old and fierce for his ten years. Since he was usually dealing with people as uninhibited as himself, men and women unacquainted with the dicta of Spock and Gesell, there were limits to his unsocial activities. Mrs. O'Hara would not hesitate to break a beer bottle over his young head; and any member of the Pereira clan from their two-year-old to a senile grandmother would carve him up first and worry about the law later.

So when Mr. Kang moved into a small house on the corner of his own street, the Demon was greatly intrigued. Here was a man who plainly didn't belong. He was neat, quiet, left no empty wine bottles in the trash heap, and lived a sedate life without even one brawl to liven the atmosphere. He was alone, and obviously had few retaliatory powers. It was even possible he might have qualms about clobbering a child.

All of this was gratifying enough, but better yet was the little man's anatomy, which was clearly alien throughout. There could be no mistake about that; the Demon had seen Mr. Kang's likeness in hundreds of cartoons and comic books. The antennae were missing, and the talons, but it was well known that Martians didn't hesitate to remove or cleverly conceal such damning appendages when spying on Earth.

Before he had been in the neighborhood a week, Mr. Kang found himself being trailed on the street by gangs of ragamuffins yelling gleefully: "Man from Mars! Martian spy!" or "Venusian, go home!"

Led by the Demon, they destroyed his flower beds, the only ones on the block, and scribbled offensive messages with paint on the side of his house. He seemed quite helpless to deal with them. Once or twice he attempted pursuit, but was ludicrously slow and clumsy. This the Demon promptly ascribed to different gravity, although his explanation was lacking in clarity as far as the gang was concerned.

But the Martian tag finally lost its savor, and their leader came up with something better. It happened on a spring morning, just after one of the Valdez children vanished. Even though she had nine others, Mrs. Valdez became hysterical. Her grief, instead of being one ninth that of a mother with only one child, paradoxically sounded more like nine-fold despair, and the whole neighborhood was soon aware of her loss.

Shortly after hearing the news, the Demon led a new foray against Mr. Kang, just missing with a decayed tomato when the little man came to his door in defense of some recently planted dahlias.

"Yah! Man from Mars!" the Demon shrieked, dancing nimbly out of his victim's reach. "Where's Jimmy Valdez? Bet he's killed little Jimmy! He's a People Eater! Kang, the People Eater!"

The phrase was irresistible. From then on, Mr. Kang was known to the gang, and in fact to most adults in the neighborhood, as "The People Eater."

In an area favored by transients, where there are many cheap boarding houses as well as flimsy cottages in peeling disrepair, there are frequent disappearances. Families vanish overnight, usually leaving small, unpaid bills, since large ones aren't permitted by the wary merchants. Boys—and girls, for that matter—from twelve on, finding their homes intolerable, run off to the nearest large city, determined not to grow up like their parents.

Every time anybody left in such a fashion, the Demon came to Mr. Kang's house. "Who ate up the Zimmels?" he would chant; and his followers, well schooled, chorused the answer: "Old Kang, the People Eater—he ate up the Zimmels, and the Reillys, and the Drakes!"

The victim was quite helpless. At first, he made the mistake of going to the parents. They were sullen and uncooperative, obviously resentful of his neatness and careful, if accented, English. Their reply to his charges was either "Boys will be boys"; or a tacit admission that the children were no longer controllable.

It was equally useless to chase them, since Mr. Kang was no match for youthful agility. He would hiss and sputter angrily through his wide frog-lips, but that only added to their fun. Certainly his enunciation was bad, and what got through the narrow opening was further distorted by a heavy accent, middle European in texture.

"He's talkin' Martian!" the Demon would yell. "Say some more, ol' People Eater! Whyn't yah go back to Mars so's they kin unnerstand?"

At the end of five weeks, even this was beginning to lose some of its appeal. Then, providentially, little Mary Hogan, aged six, vanished for real. In all the other cases—for example, that of the Valdez family—the lost member turned up sooner or later, or was heard from. But Mary was gone; she was far too young to run away, so there was no doubt a crime had been committed.

The police, even had they been greatly concerned about a slum area, were helpless. There were stories that the child had gone off in a car; others that she had been walking hand-in-hand with a small, dark man; still others that a blonde woman, expensively dressed, had taken the pretty, blue-eyed girl.

None of these accounts satisfied the Demon. He stood in front of Mr. Kang's house and shrilled: "Where's Mary Hogan? Did you eat her all up, you dirty little People Eater?" Then later, inspired by the adulation of his friends, he daringly came to the front door, and left a note which read: "Beware People Eater Im coming in soon to find Mary."

It's doubtful that he meant to be taken seriously; in this he made the mistake of other, more notable dictators who had to implement boasts they assumed would be passed over as mere pep-talks. To his gang, the Demon had unwittingly committed himself to an act of derring-do. It quickly became clear to him that unless he really faced Kang alone, in his den, the other boys would no longer accept him unquestioningly as their true leader. Instead there would be a struggle for power; and

Jesus Martinez, of the smoldering black eyes, was next in the line of succession, and very impatient. It was not certain that the Demon could whip him in a fair fight—or the other kind, either.

So, driven by circumstances, a minor Caesar at his Rubicon, the Demon swore to invade Kang's lair, there either to rescue Mary Hogan, or acquire proof of her foul murder and consumption by the People Eater.

As they congratulated him on his daring, large eyes, more yellow than brown, were watching from inside the house; and upon Mr. Kang's bland face was a strange expression, one that made him look sinister ...

That night, at eight thirty, while the gang waited outside the picket fence, which Kang rebuilt with ant-like persistence every time they tore it down, the Demon reconnoitered. Inside it was almost dark, with just a faint glow from the second bedroom near the back of the house. No doubt it was there that the Martian lurked, picking the frail bones of Mary Hogan. Well and good. If some window near the front was open, the Demon's chances were excellent. He was quite experienced at such entrances, having helped to rob three small groceries and a liquor store, which he invaded through windows too small for the adults who sponsored these operations.

Now, to his relief, a window in the dining room was half open. He could climb in, a safe distance from Kang, stall for a minute or two, and then retreat, perhaps taking something of value along. More than that he had never intended to accomplish. It was no part of his plan actually to confront the little man on home territory. After all, he was only ten, and while contemptuous of adults in general and this one in particular, the Demon was a realist. A child simply couldn't fight a grownup on his own terms; instead you used agility, guerilla tactics, and ridicule. No, the Demon would invent some exciting tale about catching the People Eater at his unnatural feast, outfacing and eluding the monster, and leaving him with empty, bloodstained talons. They wouldn't believe him; but neither would the gang dare give him the lie to his face—not after he actually broke in and robbed Kang. And, in any case, none of the others had the guts to go in and check up—not even Martinez. Sure, they knew old Kang was no Martian, and no cannibal, either, just as the Demon did; but it still took plenty of nerve to break into any house with an adult there.

Now, as he prepared to slip through the window over the low sill, Wally Johnson—stupid, loyal Wally—pressed something thick and cold into his sweaty hand.

"Here, you might need this, Demon," he mumbled.

It was his prize possession, a switchblade knife; the kind that opened to an eight-inch dagger. Pleased, the Demon wordlessly punched his disciple hard on one shoulder. Then he glided into the room, raising the sash all the way, so that he could get out in a hurry if anything went sour—a precaution his adult sponsors had taught him.

The room was dark and still. If Kang was awake in that lighted bedroom, he was awfully quiet. Perhaps one peek would do no harm. It was a cinch to outrun the guy; the window was readily available in any emergency. Besides, Kang was just a fat little oddball who probably couldn't hold the Demon even if he did catch him. More than one angry adult had found it impossible to hang on to a wiry ten-year-old who used feet, nails, teeth, and a round, hard little head all at once.

Very cautiously, his heart thumping, the boy went down the long, shadowy corridor toward the back bedroom. There were faint sounds inside; Kang was awake all right, and doing something. The Demon crept closer, and was about to put one eye to the keyhole, when the door was flung open, throwing a flood of queer greenish light into the hall. Before he could move, Kang stepped out, facing him squarely. There was something terribly different about the little man. His eyes seemed phosphorescent in their dark sockets; small antennae wriggled springily on his great bald head. He looked at the boy and smiled—a humorless shark-grin full of evil gloating. It was now clear to the Demon why Kang kept his lips together in public; for behind them was a fantastic array of huge fangs like glass splinters, running to the very back of his throat. No human dentition ever took such form.

Frozen in place by the apparition before him, the Demon heard Kang say in a thick, bubbly voice: "You were right all the time, boy. I *am* a People Eater." He raised his right hand so that the green light struck it directly; and the Demon saw a human head, one that by its colors had not been buried yesterday. The monster lifted it to his lips, and rasped a mouthful of putrefying flesh from one cheek. Then he dropped the loathsome thing, and with arms outstretched, came toward the boy. The Demon saw glittering talons that worked in and out like a cat's claws …

His paralysis broken, the boy whirled to run. Escape seemed certain; even easy; then one toe caught in a torn strand of carpeting, and the Demon tumbled to the floor. The People Eater bent over him, groping, and weird, snarly noises came from the fanged mouth. It was clearly impossible to get away now, so in his terror the Demon did what all his training and experience had prepared him for. He pressed the release button of the knife, and as the gleaming blade snapped free, jabbed upwards with all his strength.

There was a thin, gurgling cry, oddly incongruous for such a fearsome figure; then Kang crumpled, vainly clutching at his torn flesh. The Demon scrambled to his feet, and whimpering ran for the window …

"Make-up," Captain Wallace was saying. "The damnedest thing. He worked for Majestic Pictures until they got wise to his outside amusements. And all that stuff—the teeth, claws, and that crazy head with a place on one cheek for chicken meat—just props from some horror picture he made years back: 'The Mad Ghoul Strikes.' Kang was obviously trying to scare the kid; and the boy was scared, all right. That was Kang's mistake—the boy was so damn panicky he felt cornered, and just had to use the knife.

"Well, it's illegal entry; but self-defense or manslaughter, or what, God only knows. Ten years old! We'll let the little devil sweat for a while; it may be good for his soul. No hurry about telling him we found Mary Hogan buried in the basement."

Too Young to Live

The letter came just as Alan Fairchild was about to eat breakfast. He heard the click of the mailbox cover, and went out to check, expecting nothing more than the usual circulars addressed to "Occupant."

But this letter was obviously different; an airmail envelope, although, oddly enough, there was no return address. Nor did he recognize the printing of his name, which was done in a sprawling, backhand way.

As a bachelor of fifty, rather sour—Alan had to admit this, but blamed his health, in particular a worthless digestive tract—he had very few acquaintances, no close friends, and only one correspondent, a man in New Zealand with whom he had been playing a chess game by mail for three years. His parents had died years before; he was an only child, and had no relations closer than an uncle in Washington, whom he hadn't heard from in ages.

It was a small pleasure, therefore, to a man who had few, to savor this letter before opening it; to speculate and wonder a bit; even to play detective. Why airmail, which implied haste? And no return address, an omission suggestive of illegality—blackmail, poison-pen, an offer to send obscene pictures. Here Alan chuckled wryly. He was the poorest possible pickings for a blackmailer: barely enough money to live on, thanks to his stingy employers and their pitiful disability pension. As for poison-pen letters, that was a laugh; he had no contact with his neighbors; and God knows was in no position to invite envy, or indeed, any strong emotion. As for photographs, he assumed they were more often offered to adolescent boys than half-dead crocks of fifty.

The postmark, Baltimore, didn't suggest much either. He didn't know anybody who lived there; not since Aunt Jennie had died, fifteen years ago. Well, he might as well open the thing; there wasn't much more pleasure the envelope could supply. He dipped his spoon into the blob of tepid cereal and skimmed milk that had been his breakfast— how long now? Forever, it seemed; and the stuff didn't appeal to him any more now than it had at the start. While swallowing that first depressing bite, he slit the envelope with a table-knife. Unfolding the contents, he read the message, which was short and pithy. He had expected some new pitch for insurance; certainly an anti-climax, in any case, but this note changed his whole life in seconds.

That one mouthful of gruel went down, although Alan coughed and sputtered as his throat closed spasmodically. But there were no others from that bowl. Instead, after sitting there in his faded robe for thirty seconds, he gave a dry bark of a laugh, seized the dish of cereal, and with flawless aim shattered it against one scabrous wall of the kitchen. A sickly painting of three kittens playing with a ball of yarn fell with a clatter, as its cord broke. He had never cared for it; the thing had been up when he rented the apartment, and Alan had not bothered to take it down. Now it could stay on the floor. For two cents he'd wreck the whole place before leaving.

But that would take too much energy; he had a better use for what was left. He got up, went to the bathroom for a careful shave, dressed in his one remaining decent suit, which was of good material, even if out of style by six years, and put on a gaudy tie—one he'd never had the gall to wear before. It was much too sporty for a man of his age, but to hell with that.

Going to his bedroom, he pulled a shoebox out of one corner of the dusty closet, where it had been hidden under a heap of old clothes. The reserve fund, he noted, was pretty low, but adequate for present need; there were bills amounting to one hundred and seventy-eight dollars in it. He crammed them all in his wallet, joining them to a lone fiver. The empty box he left on the soiled bedspread, dust and all. Devil with cleaning up; he wouldn't be back here again. *Let them sue me,* he thought with malicious delight. That old bitch of a landlady had never given him a thing but higher monthly bills.

At the door he paused for a moment to take stock. Had he forgotten anything important? It would be a nuisance to return. Yes, there was something he ought to take along. Alan returned to the bedroom. *Where was that thing, anyhow?* He hadn't thought about it for years. In the duffel bag, most likely.

He dragged the mustard colored sack down from a high shelf, panting a little. This wasn't helping his rinky-dink heart any. The bag was dusty and stained, and had an unpleasant, moldy smell. After all, tied shut since Korea. No matter; he opened it, pawed through some filthy army fatigue clothing, and found the .45. *It better have a few shells in the magazine,* he thought; otherwise he wouldn't know where to find any. *Did sporting goods stores actually carry G.I. type ammo these days?* Good deal—the magazine held five of the blunt, metal-jacketed bullets. More than enough; no reason he should need any, but you couldn't tell. He tested the action; no cleaning or oil for years, but one thing about the Colt .45, it was rugged. You couldn't hit the rear end of an elephant at ten feet with it, but the automatic always worked. And it would stop anybody, another good point.

Alan thrust the heavy gun into his belt, well to the left side, where the coat would hide it. There was almost no chance that a cop would suddenly decide to frisk a respectable looking man on a busy street in daylight, but if that should happen—killing one of them wouldn't bother Alan too much; not just now.

He was tempted to leave the front door wide open, in the hope that some young vandals would walk in and tear up the joint. But that was pretty silly, so he locked it behind him.

Once on the street, he savored the crisp spring air. First of all breakfast; a real one; the kind he hadn't had for ten years. What was the best place around here? He was out of touch completely. Too long a period of eating at home. Then he saw a sign: "House of Pancakes." They had a fine reputation. And once he'd heard two kids talking about the pretty waitresses there. A good looking gal around didn't spoil tasty food, that was sure.

He sat in a booth, feeling an odd excitement. You'd think he was doing something really wild. The waitress was cute, at that. About nineteen, beautifully groomed; delectable figure; full above the waist;

tight, round hips; long legs. The uniform didn't hurt her at all, he reflected.

Looking up from the menu, Alan said crisply: "A big stack of wheats, sausage, bacon, and a pot of coffee."

In a sweetly patient voice, that held a hint of weariness, the girl said: "Number Three has either sausage or bacon, not both, sir."

He looked at her sharply. *Just because I'm middle-aged, balding, and no bargain, she doesn't know I'm alive,* Alan thought. *Baby,* he said to himself, *I could have you if I liked. Today, any girl around is mine. If it takes money, I can get plenty. Hell, I could even borrow from a loan shark—promise him whatever it takes. Or use the gun on somebody who's loaded. For that matter, girlie, I could even wait for you with this gun tonight, and make you come along ...* But aloud he said: "Look, miss, I don't care what's on the menu—make it a side order, or anything you like."

He guessed she was a little surprised, but too well trained or naturally aloof to show it. In any case, she noted his order, and filled it accurately.

He put five large pats of pure, yellow butter on the stack of cakes, and then drenched the whole heap with genuine maple syrup, evidently one of their specialties. He ate very slowly, sure that his stomach must be shrunk, and anxious to postpone the inevitable heartburn. *Must be two thousand calories right on this plate,* he thought; *and enough saturated fat to clog the arteries of a yearling bull. But, man, it tastes good. Those physiologists who proved with starved rats that food came ahead of sex, have it just right.*

Alan took eighty minutes to clean his plate. He left a big tip, knowing the waitress had him pegged as an old sourpuss who wouldn't leave much. *I might come back for you tonight,* he promised her silently, and left.

It was now after ten, thanks to his sleeping so late; but then lounging in bed was one of the few pleasures still left to him. As for time between now and lunch—and he was already planning the menu—a walk in the spring sunshine, and then a dozen drinks in as many bars, but carefully spaced. It wouldn't do to get stoned, not this early in the day.

In each bar, Alan had one of the drinks he'd missed so long, favoring the most exotic ones, and counting on his fat-lined stomach to keep him reasonably sober. First a martini, then a pousse-café, then brandy, then creme de menthe—it was a fantastic sequence, but nothing could stop him today. Maybe the alcohol even helped counter the fat in his bloodstream, he hoped, while sipping a bloody mary.

For lunch he went to a luxury spot, where his clothes made a few eyebrows go up. There he had French food: onion soup, with cheese and delectable croutons, duckling in orange sauce, fresh asparagus soaked in melted butter, and the richest of pastry, buried in liquid chocolate. How he'd missed chocolate. "Poison," the doctor had said; "all the wrong kind of fat; it'll kill you dead." Well, the doctor was wrong—no amount of chocolate could kill Alan Fairchild. Just to prove the point, he managed to drink a malted at four-thirty. He was delighted at the way his stomach stood the gaff. That was quite a break.

Even more remarkable was the way his appetite returned again at eight. It was as if his body wanted to make up for those years of savorless, tepid meals. "Don't ever eat anything, even a light snack, after six," the doctor had warned him. Well, the Powers That Be—all of them quite mad, of course; just take a good look at the world—were on Alan's side right now; the medicine man represented a lost cause.

So at eight in the evening, Alan disposed of lobster fondue, with heavy beer, followed by chocolate pie under real whipped cream. He didn't eat quite as much as for lunch, but enjoyed every bit. Perhaps his stomach and digestive tract were too stunned by the avalanche of rich foods, but there was no heartburn; in fact, Alan felt fine.

At ten he was in a neighborhood bar; nothing plushy this time. He sat in a booth, alone, sipping creme de cacao; chocolate never did pall on him, and there were many years to recover. Somebody put a coin in the jukebox; the music was loud and unpleasant to Alan's ears. He preferred Friml and Herbert; this rock and roll was unbearable. When the same man, a big, husky fellow, with mean little eyes, dropped in several quarters for a long run of the stuff, Alan yelled from the booth: "Turn that damned junk off; don't you have any taste at all?"

The tall man strode over very truculently, and said: "Nobody asked you, wise guy. You bucking for a knuckle sandwich?"

For a moment Alan shrank back; he had never been a fighter, and this ape obviously could pull off his arms and legs without straining himself. Then he remembered the gun, and snatched it out. At the sight of it, the big man turned pale.

"Look," he said, in a voice that quavered, "I didn't mean nothing." He turned to the bartender whose mouth was open. "Hey, Harry, what kind of a place is this? You play a little music, and somebody pulls a gun."

"Never mind; I'm going," Alan said huskily. This wasn't really a good spot to start shooting; nothing to gain. At the door he glared at the dozen people in the place, and said, hoping to sound convincing: "And don't follow me or call the police. If you do—" He waved the .45.

Once in the street again, he paused irresolute. No more food; he'd had it. The image of the cool, subtly disdainful waitress returned. There was just a possibility she'd be going off duty about now; the mad gods would see to that, this being his night.

And the mad gods came through. When the girl left the restaurant, Alan was waiting. He followed her to her car, and as she was about to get in, showed her the gun.

"Don't make a sound," he warned, "or I'll kill you." He meant it, a fact which surprised Alan himself, and his voice must have made it plain to the girl, because she was too terrified to scream. Instead she gasped: "It's you—you, this morning in the restaurant ..."

"That's right, it's me. Drive me to your place. Do you live alone?"

"Yes—that is, no. The girl I share an apartment with is there; and lots of people come by—"

"You're lying," he said calmly, certain it was so. "But I won't take any chances. Drive to Magnolia Circle, up in the hills."

"I won't—please, let me go."

He put the muzzle of the gun to her ear.

"Drive. I mean it. I'll kill you."

Weeping, she followed his directions. The busy part of the city was soon left behind. *On a weeknight,* he thought coldly, *Magnolia Circle will be deserted. Yet the night is pleasant. And she's a very pretty girl. Not so damned haughty, now.* This would be the end of a perfect day … a complete day.

When they reached a lonely spot up in the hills, he ordered her out of the car, ignoring her sobs and pleas. He forced her, at gunpoint, to a grassy bank, heavy with the scent of some night-blooming wildflowers.

"Here we are," he said pleasantly. "I don't have to tell you what comes next."

She was sobbing wildly now, but he felt no pity, rather his excitement grew. Anticipation and imagination were stirring him up to an unbelievable pitch. He exulted in that; there was some juice in the old carcass yet, by God! Here, too, he was many years behind. The mad gods had been cruel to him; why should he have pity?

Pointing the gun right at her face, a pale blur in the moonlight, he raised her chin with his other hand, and put his lips to hers. Her mouth was cool and damp; he felt her shrink at the contact. Angry, he stepped back, and said: "Shall I play lady's maid, or will you take off your own clothes?"

"No—please, please—don't make me—"

But he closed in again, gun forward, to claw at her bodice. His heart was thumping madly, madly at the touch of warm flesh—until it reached a crescendo and exploded in a cataract of pain. The .45 dropped from his hand, which clutched at his chest. He strained tall for a moment, then fell to the ground. With a whimpering cry, the girl ran; in seconds she was lost in the gloom.

"Little fool," Alan muttered. "What's the use of running?"

The pain subsided slightly, but he was getting numb; the end must be near. He heard the letter crackle in his breast pocket, where his hand pressed his chest.

Things were growing dim; all he could see now was the letter, with fiery words dancing in his brain. No salutation and, of course, no signature:

Massive exchange of nuclear missiles *absolutely certain* within 24 hours after you get this. Don't tell anybody, but find a hole. I doubt if that will help; both sides are using 200-megaton warheads. God save us all.

Checklist of Sources

Note: The checklist below gives the original publication source for each of the stories included in this collection.

"Heat"
Bestseller Mystery Magazine, September 1960

"The Glint"
Alfred Hitchcock's Mystery Magazine, December 1965

"The Reason"
Cavalier, July 1967 (this story appeared here as "The False Face")

"Born to Save"
Alfred Hitchcock's Mystery Magazine, September 1964

"The Price of a Princess"
The London Mystery Selection, No. 63, December 1964

"Chain Smoker"
Alfred Hitchcock's Mystery Magazine, August 1965

"Swan Song"
Adam, February 1966

"A Small Favor"
Bestseller Mystery Magazine, January 1960

"Bet with a Witch"
Fling, December 1963

"A Change for the Better"
Alfred Hitchcock's Mystery Magazine, December 1963

"The Emperor's Dogs"
Bizarre! Mystery Magazine, November 1965 (this story appeared here under the pseudonym Abel Jacobi)

"Mr. Kang vs. the Demon"
Alfred Hitchcock's Mystery Magazine, November 1961

"Too Young to Live"
Off Beat Detective Stories, May 1963

About the Author

Arthur Porges was born in Chicago, Illinois on August 20, 1915. One of four brothers, he was educated at Roosevelt High School and Senn High School before enrolling at The Lewis Institute where he achieved a Bachelor of Science Degree in Mathematics. After the successful completion of his postgraduate studies, through which he attained Masters Degrees in Mathematics and Engineering from the Illinois Institute of Technology, Porges enlisted in the U.S. Army in 1942. During the Second World War he served as an artillery instructor, teaching algebra and trigonometry to field personnel. He was stationed at various military installations including Camp White in Oregon, Fort Sill, Oklahoma, Camp Roberts, California and at Barnes Hospital in Vancouver, Washington. After the war Porges returned to Illinois and taught mathematics at the Western Military Academy, going on to serve as an assistant professor at De Paul University. Having taught at Occidental College in Los Angeles for a brief stint in the late forties, Porges made a permanent move to California in 1951 and spent several years as a mathematics teacher at Los Angeles City College. During this period he wrote and sold short stories as a sideline. In 1957, Porges retired from teaching to write full-time. He went on to publish hundreds of short stories in numerous magazines and newspapers. Many of his stories appeared in *Alfred Hitchcock's Mystery Magazine*, *Ellery Queen's Mystery Magazine*, *Amazing Stories* and *The Magazine of Fantasy and Science Fiction*. His fiction spanned several genres, with tales ranging from science fiction and fantasy to horror, mysteries, and so on. At his most prolific his work was appearing in three or four periodicals in one month alone. Among his best-known stories are "The Ruum," "The Rats," "No Killer Has Wings," "The Mirror" and "The Rescuer." Thirteen previous book collections of his short stories have been published: *Three Porges Parodies and a Pastiche* (1988), *The Mirror and Other Strange Reflections* (2002), *Eight Problems in Space: The Ensign De Ruyter Stories* (2008), *The Adventures of Stately Homes and Sherman Horn*

(2008), *The Calabash of Coral Island and Other Early Stories* (2008), *The Miracle of the Bread and Other Stories* (2008), *The Devil and Simon Flagg and Other Fantastic Tales* (2009), *The Curious Cases of Cyriack Skinner Grey* (2009), *The Ruum and Other Science Fiction Stories* (2010), *The Rescuer and Other Science Fiction* Stories (2014), *Unusual Plants of the Galaxy* (2014), *No Killer Has Wings: The Casebook of Dr. Joel Hoffman* (2017) and *These Daisies Told: The Casebook of Professor Ulysses Price Middlebie* (2018). A keen birdwatcher and an avid reader, in later years Porges wrote many articles, essays and poems, most of which were published in the *Monterey Herald*. Several of his poems were collected in the book *Spring, 1836: Selected Poems* (2008). After spells in Laguna Beach and San Clemente, Porges moved north, eventually settling in Pacific Grove. He passed away, at the age of 90, in May 2006.